D1458203

LOVE STRUCK

C0000 002 383 623

Look out for Rachael s first novel:

Who doesn t want to star in the world s greatest romance?

"A story of modern romance that will leave you warm and tingly all over"

RACHAEL WING

LOVE STRUCK

📖 SCHOLASTIC

HOUNSLOW LIBRARIES	
C0000 002 383 623	
PETERS	01-Dec-2008
CF	£5.99
	HOU

First published in the UK in 2008 by Scholastic Children's Books
An imprint of Scholastic Ltd
Euston House, 24 Eversholt Street
London, NW1 1DB, UK
Registered office: Westfield Road, Southam, Warwickshire, CV47 0RA
SCHOLASTIC and associated logos are trademarks
and or registered trademarks of Scholastic Inc.

Text copyright © Rachael Wing, 2008
The right of Rachael Wing to be identified as the
author of this work has been asserted by her.
Cover illustration © Tim Spencer, 2008

ISBN 978 1407 1074 3 1

British Library Cataloguing-in-Publication Data
A CIP catalogue record for this book is available from the British Library
All rights reserved
This book is sold subject to the condition that it shall not, by way of
trade or otherwise, be lent, hired out or otherwise circulated in any form
of binding or cover other than that in which it is published. No part of this
publication may be reproduced, stored in a retrieval system, or transmitted in
any form or by any means (electronic, mechanical, photocopying, recording
or otherwise) without the prior written permission of Scholastic Limited.

Typeset by M Rules
Printed by CPI Bookmarque, Croydon, CR0 4TD
Papers used by Scholastic Children's Books are
made from wood grown in sustainable forests.

1 3 5 7 9 10 8 6 4 2

This is a work of fiction. Names, characters, places, incidents and dialogues are
products of the author's imagination or are used fictitiously. Any resemblance to
actual people, living or dead, events or locales is entirely coincidental.

www.scholastic.co.uk/zone

For Mum and for Hannah.
Thank you Grandma and Grandmum for boosting sales,
Matticus for enthusiasm, and to the rest of the
family and my friends for their support.
(Thanks to you for buying this book! Enjoy!)

Oh, and ta for the muffin joke, Canty.
A crab walks into a bar . . .

1

"Well, if it isn't Little Miss Hockers. . ."

At the sound of that voice I jumped out of my skin, and skilfully fell (well, actually it was more of a severe nose dive that sent me lurching head first) into the carrot crate. Trying to ignore the pain, and desperately trying to recover what little dignity I had left, I sat up. A little too quickly. My head collided with a spectacular elegance and poise into the shelf above, at which point I could have sworn I would never be able to think again. All other thoughts leaked out of the gaping crater now in my skull, leaving one resounding syllable that Mum would kill me for thinking, let alone crying out in agony.

It was at this point that I collapsed to the ground, clutching my head and groaning in what could have been a perfect damsel-in-distress-type way, if I hadn't sounded so much like a wounded walrus. Over my moans, I could just hear a throaty chuckle as Jonah bent down beside me and took my hands in his, away from what was left of my battered head and into bliss. His grip was soothing and strong, and I instantly melted inside; my usual reaction to his skin touching mine.

"Woah – I know I'm a god, Hockers, but there's really no need to faint at my feet; people are staring. . ."

I opened my eyes slowly, as if stirring attractively from some incredibly painful dream, and even though my vision was hazy, Jonah was the most beautiful, blurry thing I'd ever seen in my life. But then I remembered that he hadn't called or texted once since *that* night, and his perfect (but evil) face came sharply into focus. That manly, strong jaw and gorgeous mouth, and the lip ring (hmm, lip ring); the black mop of hair, all tousled like he'd fallen out of bed; those long, thick lashes that I could never get, even with the most expensive mascara known to girlkind, and, of course, those most deadly addictive, brightly green, gold-flecked eyes that a fifteen-year-old girl could get completely lost in.

When in that moment, so it came to pass,
Holly waked, and straight away loved an ass.

Damn right he was an ass, but those eyes just took every last breath out of my body – every single time.

"I've broken my brain!" I grumbled, as I faintly realized that those eyes obviously whisked away my common sense as well as my vital necessities for life. He chuckled again – that yummy

2

chuckle that made my heart shiver like it had suddenly been caught in a draft – and let go of my hands to examine my head. His hands on my head had me thinking that I was going to pass out all over again.

"Nope, nothing broken, no brain leaking out; you're still in one piece. You'll live to save the world another day, Comic Book Kid."

If you ask around in my town for a "Holly Hockers: a fourth-year girl, medium height, medium build, darkish hair and stupid laugh, who likes to hang out at Ozzie's after school and can always be found with her iPod, jamming away to The Faeries, at any time day or night", I'm pretty sure that even with that detailed description, not one person would know to point me out. The crazy thing is that if you ask the first teenager you see on the high street where you can find the "Comic Book Kid", it will be me they'll take you straight to.

Almost every kid who goes to Cathen Comp knows about Ozzie's Ice Cream Parlour. It's sacrilege not to. I don't know how everyone else found out about it, but I've been going there since I was tiny, pretty much since it was open. Mum and Dad used to take me for a treat at the end of the week, if I'd been a "good girl" – "A sundae on a Sunday!" she'd say, and I'd giggle myself stupid – but that was before Dad starting working a lot, and Mum started writing, and our sundae Sundays became fewer and fewer. So because it's only around the corner, I would go there by myself. Ozzie knew me and my parents by this time, and he and his wife, Nerin, took me into the parlour when my mum couldn't. I would taste delicious spoonfuls of his new inventions,

3

and tell him if it should be his special – there was always a different special each week. That still goes on now; sometimes the old ones are repeated, but Ozzie still comes up with crazy new concoctions too, and all of us Cathen kids love them.

When I was at the parlour, to pass the time between spoonfuls, I would draw. Ozzie would always have a paper and crayons ready. There was this painting that he had, just the one, of a black woman walking through a whirling circle of multicoloured water towards the sun, the calm sea in front of her, her hair flying back in the breeze. It was so beautiful; I would stare for ages until I couldn't remember what I was looking at.

One day a couple of years ago, I turned up, took my usual space at the gleaming silver serving bar and saw that my favourite picture wasn't there. Ozzie said he had taken it upstairs to his flat above the shop, because it didn't seem right in the parlour any more, and joked that maybe I should paint something to fill its space.

So I did. Only I thought about it, thought about what I would want to look at if I were a teenage kid waiting for ice cream, and a comic strip seemed ideal. And so H'y Girl was born (yes, H'y Girl was me, I wasn't overly imaginative with names back then) – a SuperGirl who liked eating ice cream and fighting crime (obviously not at the same time, she's not THAT super). I showed it to Ozzie, who LOVED it, and we printed it up big and stuck it in the water woman's place and it pretty much instantly became a hit.

So I began to draw one every few months, and when I met my best friend, Wes (and the Adventures of H'y Girl and Lameboy

4

started), I'd do one every few weeks, and Ozzie would display them proudly, not just on one wall, but all of them. People would say: "Ozzie, the cartoons are so cool, who did them?" and he'd reply by pointing at me and saying, "Our very own comic book kid!", and so it stuck. In Cathen Town I am just the Comic Book Kid, and nothing more.

Jonah Jones, however, is a god.

"C'mon, let me help you up. . ."

Once again his amazing hands picked me up and helped me to my feet. I drew it out as long as possible to keep him close. I know I sound a bit full on but seriously, that's how gorgeous he was — I wanted him close all the time, especially since he kissed me at the last gig. . .

I got to my feet gingerly and touched my head. It was banging like a church bell too early on a Sunday morning but I smiled anyway, just because Jonah was smiling at me. I looked down at the mess I had made of the carrot box and apple shelf and felt a pink rush to my cheeks. I wish I didn't blush so much.

"Sorry for making a mess," I apologized. "I'm not usually so . . . clumsy! Do you want me to help clear it up?"

His eyes flicked over the damage my head had done.

"Nah, don't worry, it'll give me something to do later. This place gets deader than a morgue later on, and if I have nothing to do, the old dears make me mop."

He nodded over to the two grannies with matching blue rinses at the tills. They were tutting and whispering in my direction. Oh, great, just what I needed — tutting geriatrics on my tail.

"So," Jonah said, looking straight at me. "What've you been up to? Haven't really seen you since the gig . . ."

The gig where we had that really, *really* amazing kiss, I gave you my number and you didn't text or call or anything?!

". . . yeah, I lost your number and haven't really seen you around."

So that's why he didn't text.

This glimmer of hope at the end of what seemed like a long, earthy tunnel, made my insides lurch. But I decided to play it cool. I wasn't going to get him by letting him know I'd been sat around, waiting for a text from him to say that he wants me to be his one and only girlfriend and that he thinks I'm the most gorgeous girl in school. No, I had to be the Ice Maiden. Ice Queen. Think mean; aloof.

"Oh, the gig. Yeah. Completely forgot about that! I've been so busy, like, doing homework –" I inwardly cringed "– and baby sitting –" It got worse "– and, errm, just doing some shifts at Ozzie's. . ." Oh, my sparkling social life! ". . .to get the money for my MSR ticket."

That last bit sounded better, like I was some kind of martyr for music. He smiled and my knees went weak. I casually leant against the wall to prop myself up a little, but he didn't seem to notice.

"You're going to Midsummer Rave?" he asked, interested. I nodded. His smile widened. "Me too. My dad got me a ticket for my birthday. I went last year and that was awesome. But its going to be pretty good this year, you know, with Cubical and The Dandys . . . and did you hear that at midnight—"

"The Faeries are doing their set?" I smiled then. Of course I knew that. You won't find a bigger Faeries fan than me. Well, except Wes. I think we almost class as stalkers.

"Oh yeah, I forgot that you're their number one fan," he smirked. "I suppose you're going with Wes, Sloaney and Crony?"

Margo "Sloaney" Stone (Wes's twin) and her boyfriend, Finn (yes, her "Crony"), are coming with me and Wes to the Rave. We've got a four-man tent and we're sharing it. It's only two nights, so I don't have to put up with her annoying elocution for too long. It's a wonder that Wes has turned out like he has, coming from his family. "Sloaney" doesn't even cover it.

I rolled my eyes. "Yeah, we're sharing with them, but don't call them that, they're not *that* bad. . ."

He raised his eyebrows as if to say "Yeah, right!" and carried on. "I don't know where I'm staying yet, but if you're going, maybe I'll see you there. . .?"

His eyes were magical. Like they seriously just cast a spell on me. I swear if he asked me to do the mopping for him I would do it in a second – just find me a mop! So of course I said:

"Yeah, definitely! Be there or be square!"

I just shouldn't speak to human beings.

He chuckled, bemused, as if he didn't know what to say. I wasn't surprised; I couldn't think of what to say to that either. No one has said that phrase seriously for about thirty years. This is what those eyes do to me! It was time to make a swift exit.

I leaned away from the wall and flashed him my best smile. "Well, I've got to go! See you later."

I bent down, picked up my bag from the rubble of carrots and headed for the door.

"Wait—"

I turned around slowly.

"Do I get your number then?"

My head exploded once again, this time definitely with pleasure. Pulse racing? Check. Vision swimming? Check. Head pounding? Check, check, check.

So I gave him my number before I passed out, and headed for the door.

"So I guess I'll see you around!" he called after me.

I nodded. "See you at school."

"Yeah," he grinned, those green eyes wrinkling at the corners when he smiled. "Be there or be square. . ."

I smiled, turned out of the door into the summer heat of the street and let my smile drop into a wince. What was my mind thinking and where did it go?! As I started walking down the street towards Ozzie's, I pulled my phone out of my bag and hit speed dial one.

"Yes, Hols?"

"Ozzie's. Chocolate. Ice cream. Now."

"Give me ten minutes and I'm all yours."

That's why Wes is the best friend I've ever had.

2

*N*ot many people know that Wes's real name is actually Winston. Winston Edward Stone, named after a prime minister, then a monarch, then his generations-old name that screams money in this town. The Stone Manor is the other side of town from us, on the richest street in Cathen town. When Mum found out that was where he lived, she laughed in disbelief.

"Wes lives on Millionare's Row? *Our* Wes?"

Its true; to look at him, you wouldn't think he was loaded. I mean, he doesn't exactly flaunt it like those rich Cali kids on *The O.C.* – just regular jeans, shirts, a messenger bag. But when you get a bit closer you can see the little things: that his cute, square glasses are actually Armani, that he uses some amazing

French scent that's really light and clean-smelling, and that his hair, however much he tries to mess it up, is cut by Toni and Guy. *The* Toni and Guy – they take it in turns. Yes, this boy is loaded, but he doesn't act like it. Like, he chose to come to Cathen Comp instead of a posh-lads' school, because he didn't want to "play 'rugger' all day and come home with a posh accent", and he dresses from the high street like any other guy our age, even though his mother plies him with designer shirts and chinos every week. And you can hold many a conversation with him and never once will you see that he already has about three times the amount of money that I will ever have in my life. He's just a normal, down to earth, nice guy. Who likes music.

Music is how we met – we chose to carry on music in our third year and just happened to be put next to each other in our class. Just before class started I was sat with my headphones in, listening to my favourite song – "Love in Idleness" by The Faeries – full blast; he happened to catch the beat and started tapping along to it. When it got to the chorus and we started singing simultaneously, each of us knew that the other was a friend for life.

Now, almost two years on, he's still my best friend. I don't know what I would do without him, to be perfectly honest. Which is why I was sat at the shiny bar of Ozzie's heaving parlour, waiting for him to sort me out and help me eat some pretty fantastic ice cream.

"Beautiful Holly, how can Uncle Ozzie help you out today, eh?" Ozzie's Turkish accent hasn't left him, even though he's been living here longer than I've been alive. He's a pretty amazing guy – speaks four languages fluently, a few conversationally, owns his own business, has a lovely wife (who makes the best Turkish food ever!) and also, he looks out for me and Mum. It's like having an uncle just around the corner.

"Ohh, I don't know – what's the new special?" I asked, scanning the various flavours in front of me.

He smiled wickedly. "It's your favourite. . ."

"Butterscotch and Malteaser?!"

"How big?" he laughed, heading for the cupboard.

"Wes is coming in a minute, so make it a large," I smiled, watching him take a huge bowl from the cupboard. He started to scoop large spoonfuls out of the vat of ice cream before him, and looked me straight in the eyes.

"Ahh, Mister Stone is coming!" I knew what was coming after this. He says it every time I come here. "So when are you and him finally going to get together, eh?"

I rolled my eyes, but laughed too. "How many times, Ozzie – he's my best friend! It's a no-go!"

He put down his spoon and pointed at the nearest cartoon strip of "H'y Girl and Lameboy", a particular favourite of mine where the superheroes have a dance-off against the cast of *High School Musical*, who have become quite evil. He stared at the poster, then cast his glance to me. "I don't believe it!" he cried. He shook his head, looking back down at his ice cream, ladling another spoonful into the bowl. "You kids are crazy; you don't even see what is right in front of your eyes! But then *love looks not with the eyes, but with the mind* – so if you say it's a 'no-go', then I cannot argue, eh?"

He chuckled as he went over to the sprinkle station and covered my serving with thick chocolate fudge sauce and then multicoloured sprinkles. I was so busy drooling rather attractively that I hardly noticed Wes saunter into the parlour. He was wearing his favourite shirt – a blue tee with the legend "Goodfellow is my God" across the back – his dark hair styled "to look messy". I don't really understand why boys do that. Why can't they just go with the fluffy, rolled-out-of-bed look? Wes says that he doesn't like it, but it looks so soft and cute without product. I'm probably the only person to ever see his hair like that; he never goes out without styling first. He's more of a chick than I am. In his tattered jeans and flip-flops, he sat down in the chair next to me, eyed the bowl of gooey mess that had just been set before me, and then beamed at our dealer.

"Butterscotch and malteaser – Ozzie, you ledge!" Ozzie laughed as Wes grabbed a spoon and took a bite, then grinned and gave Ozzie two thumbs up and continued to shovel his face full of ice cream. What an attractive boy.

"So," he declared, with a mouth full of fudge sauce, "what's going on, H?"

Ozzie turned away to serve another customer in the long queue of impatient teens waiting for a fix of his lush frozen ambrosia, and I turned to my friend and pushed aside my fringe.

"Do I have a bruise coming?" I asked, and Wes put down his spoon to have a look.

"No," he said after a quick inspection. "Not yet. Why?"

I picked up my spoon and tucked in before starting my most current tale of embarrassment and woe.

12

"Well, I just went to the greengrocers' –"

"– oooh, for the first time since –"

"– the gig, yeah. And so I went in, because I thought everything was clear and that he wasn't working; so I bent down to root around the carrots –"

"– *nice* –".

"And then I heard this voice, all deep and gorgeous, saying, 'Well, if it isn't Little Miss Hockers' and I nearly died – there I was bending over a pile of old carrots, my big bum waving around in the air –"

"– it's not *that* big –"

"Oh, cheers!" I laughed, and he laughed too, his nose wrinkling as he chuckled. "Well, my rear, however big, was waving around and he scared me so much that I fell flat into the tub of carrots, and then when I tried to stand up and got hit by a face in the shelf – I mean shelf in the face—" By this time Wes was hooting with laughter like a small owl, and I had to give him a small shove on the shoulder, because his giggles were making me giggle, and turning my tragedy into a comedy. "And it was just so embarrassing that I had to get out of there quick as a cat, without any carrots, and then I rang you. . ."

"Oh dear," he sighed, shaking his head through subsiding chuckles, then his conker-coloured eyes met mine as he ate the luscious dessert. "Not a good day for Cathen's leading superhero, eh?" I shook my head, carefully touching the point where my head had nearly split in two, and helped myself to some more ice cream. We're so greedy; the bowl was nearly finished.

"No," I agreed. "Getting publicly humiliated? Bad times. But the hottest guy in school —" Wes uttered a sarcastic, pointed cough. "— asking for my number again after said public humiliation? Good times!"

"He didn't say that he lost your number, did he?" Wes asked sardonically. I didn't say anything and looked at the floor. "Hols, that's the oldest line in the book! I'm telling you, he's not good enough for you; the guy's a sleaze."

I frowned. "He might have actually lost my number, you know. Don't be so cynical! And don't ruin this for me; you know I've liked him for ages!"

Wes rolled his eyes. "Only because 'he's just *so* gorgeous!' — and you call me superficial?"

"You're just jealous!" I declared, nicking the last bit of ice cream from the bowl. "Anyway, he said he's going to MSR, so even if he doesn't call I'll see him there!" I pushed the spoon around the bowl, preparing to tell Wes about my plan. "He also said that he didn't have a tent to stay in for the weekend. . ."

I bit my lip and waited for Wes to respond. After a few seconds he looked up, saw my face, and realized what I was asking. "You've got to be joking! Hols, I can't stand the guy for a double maths, let alone two nights." I pouted, doing my best wounded-puppy face, but it's kind of lost its effect after two years. He shook his head. "Sorry, Comic Book Kid, but you'll have to woo and win him some other way. . ."

I carried on pouting. "Fine, be like that. But if it was the other way around I would have said yes!"

"No, you wouldn't. And besides, it would never be the other way around; I prefer the tall, blonde and beautiful type."

I laughed. "Whatever, Winston. It was worth asking. But if a beautiful girl did walk in here right now, and you totally fell for her, I would ask her myself to share our tent."

Wes was staring straight over my shoulder towards the door with a glazed expression.

"It makes me feel so loved when you don't listen to a word I say. . ."

Wes's eyes clicked back up to mine.

"Her."

"What?" I said, totally baffled.

He nodded to the door, his eyes now fixed back on it. "Her."

I turned in my seat and did a double take. I could have sworn I'd just seen Barbie. I looked again. Yes, I had seen Barbie. Real Life Barbie. Swishy blonde hair, tiny shorts, four-season tan: Barbie.

Barbie took off her shades and looked around the parlour at all the people inside. She saw the bar and walked straight over to it. Swish, swish with her shiny hair. She was pretty tall, too. Well, anything is tall to my measley 5′3″, but even by normal standards, this chick was tall.

"It's your turn to be joking, mate," I whispered to Wes, who was still pretty much gaping at The Plastic One as if she were made of gold. "Jeez! Shut your mouth, why don't you? You look like the Channel Tunnel."

He didn't hear me, his eyes fixed on the girl.

"She's coming this way! Act like you're not my girlfriend."

15

I frowned incredulously. "But I'm *not* your girlfriend!"

Barbie, now at the bar just behind Wes, cast me a strange look, then turned back to the ice cream. She was OK-looking up close. Well, actually, she was pretty much ten million times better than OK-looking. Surprise surprise, she had bright blue eyes and really white teeth. She was like a perfect advertisement for Sweden, so I was mildly surprised when a wholly different accent came out of her mouth.

"Hi, do you, like, have any sorbets, or frozen yoghurt?"

I felt like shouting, "It's 'yog-urt' for one, not 'youh-guurrt'; and no, this is an *ice cream* parlour, we do ice cream!", but I kept my mouth shut. I often get angry at people who are prettier than me, but it's not their fault, so I just have to be bitter and hostile inside instead, and come across as a nice, non-shallow person to everyone not inside my head.

Ozzie smiled at her and shook his head. "I am very sorry, we have not any frozen yoghurt, only sorbet in the corner."

Barbie smiled her (100-watt) smile, thanked Ozzie (who winked at the awestruck Wes, then went back to serving), and wandered over to the far end of the freezer-server to have a look at the flavours. Wes turned around to have another look, then turned back to me with an expression on his face that just said, "Hamana!": meaning, "Man, that girl is hot; I would!"

As Wes looked like he was so in awe he wouldn't speak for a good few minutes, I thought it best to ask him nod/shake questions.

"You like?"

Nod.

16

"You want?"

Nod nod.

"You need my help to get?"

Nod nod nod.

I grinned.

"Well, Stoney, it looks like your dormant hormones have actually awakened! Congrats and such. What's the plan, big man?"

His expression of delirious happiness was as frozen as the ice cream surrounding us, but it broke as he squeaked, "A name, please, find out her name."

I rolled my eyes dramatically and slid off my stool, then wandered over to the American beauty deliberating over which low-fat treat to have. I wondered briefly if she knew that the sorbets may be low fat, but they have more sugar in than I even want to know about, but I pushed it aside, pinned on my best smile and pointed at the Mango Lemon Twist.

"That's probably the best one in here if you're looking for a sorbet; it leaves a really nice aftertaste. It's actually my favourite, second best to the special."

I gestured to the sign that declared Butterscotch and Malteasers to be the special for the week. The doll-a-like smiled (which nearly blinded me) and nodded.

"I'll try it, thanks!" She placed an order "to go" with Nerin and then turned back to me. "I guess that would be my favourite too, but I'd never know – I'm lactose intolerant."

My jaw dropped.

Lactose intolerant?

How does this girl LIVE?!

"Bummer," I said quite coolly for a girl who was having a heart attack inside. "That's a shame." A shame? It's a catastrophe! "But the sorbets really are good, so at least you're not denied all frozen pleasures." As she laughed, my internal green-eyed monster growled again. She even had a pretty laugh, all infectious and cute. Grrr. "I'm Holly, by the way, and I pretty much live in here, hence all the ice-cream-related knowledge."

"I'm Emily," she laughed, looking around the room again. "And obviously don't know anything about ice cream! But this place is totally amped!"

"Totally what?"

Emily looked back at me, and smiled. "Oh, amped – it's like . . . cool?"

"Oh, right," I grinned. Americans have weird words. "So you're from America, right? I haven't seen you around; are you here on holiday?"

"Well, actually, I've just moved here. My mom's just gotten a new job, so we moved over for that."

"That sucks," I said, frowning. I would hate to leave Cathen just because Mum or Dad got a new job. I'd have to leave Ozzie's, and school, and no way could I leave Wes behind; he's my right arm! I began to feel sorry for her, even though she was hotter than fire. "How old are you?"

"Fifteen. Sixteen in the fall!"

"You're my year then. Are you going to Cathen Comp?"

"Yeah, I'm – oh, thanks!" She gracefully took her sorbet from Nerin, paid, then turned back to me. "I'm actually starting tomorrow. My mom says it'll help me to settle in if I meet

18

everyone now, and I might make some friends for the summer."

I nodded, my mind thinking a mile a minute. "It's my school. So what form are you going to be in, do you know?"

Squinting, she tried to remember. "Uh, 10B, I think. . ."

Our form. I had to stop myself from laughing; Wes was going to have a coronary.

"Cool, that's our form! Me and my friend Wes, that's him there, come and meet him."

I motioned over my shoulder to where Wes was, shredding a napkin, and I rolled my eyes. Couldn't he be doing something to make him look cool, like texting or something? I made a mental reminder to teach him how to look good in front of people you're trying to impress. I know I'm not an expert, what with the carrot massacre and everything, but goodness knows I know more than he does, obviously.

We walked over to The Socially Awkward One and he looked up at Emily with a bit of a dazed expression on his face.

"This is Emily."

You could see the name pass into his brain and just swirl around, taking up all the space that was before occupied with thoughts on how to talk to human beings. He just nodded.

I took a deep breath and soldiered on.

"She's just moved here from America," I explained, trying not to sound too much like a primary-school teacher.

"Hey," she said with her killer smile. "How're ya doing?"

Wes looked like he couldn't believe she was talking to him, then suddenly snapped into life.

"Yeah, I'm good, thanks, and yourself?"

19

She smiled straight into his eyes.

"I'm all the better for meeting you."

I raised my internal eyebrows. Was that a *line*?! Or did it literally just mean that she was glad that she met him? Americans are friendly, so that might just have been her being nice, or it could have been—

But I didn't have time to analyze her body language or anything like that, because as quick as a flash she said:

"Oh my gosh, look at the time! I gotta get going! See ya at school, have a nice day!"

And with a wave, she turned on her flip-flops and ran (with more agility than I'll ever possess) out of the door, and the bell on top jingled as it shut behind her.

I turned back to Wes, who was still staring at the door.

"So?" I asked, smirking at his awestruck face.

He couldn't speak for a second, then managed to force out a word.

"Emily."

"Yes. That's her name, I'm glad you picked that up."

"She's American."

"Yes."

"She's blonde."

"Yes."

"She's gorgeous."

"Meh, I suppose if you're into that whole plastic-looking thing, yeah. . ."

"And she's moved here . . . to Cathen . . . to our school?"

"Our form, in fact."

He paused for a second.

"God is rewarding me for all of my good deeds, he's sent her to me."

I cracked a mocking smile. "You don't do good deeds! You don't even do your own washing up! Juanita your maid does it! And you're not religious!"

He came out of his saintly daydream and frowned at me.

"I do!"

"Oh yeah, Lameboy, name one!"

"I . . . erm, I . . . I . . . brought you ice cream when you had that stomach bug and couldn't come to school, a few months ago!" he finished triumphantly.

"I couldn't eat it, I was being sick!" I laughed. "I had to sit and watch you eat it all, whilst I wasn't allowed to eat anything or else I'd throw up!"

That got him.

"It was still a good deed. . ." he grumbled, backing down. He looked me straight in the eyes. "Well, if God didn't send her to me, she must just be a very lucky coincidence." He put on the hopeful eyes and gently tugged my sleeve. "Will you help me? You know I'm useless at everything."

I thought about it for a second.

Then I had a genius idea.

"Can Jonah stay in the tent?"

Wes's eyes narrowed, and he put on his best John Wayne impression. "So you want to play dirty, Hockers?" I nodded. He shrugged. "Fine. I'll think about it."

I grinned and gave him a bear hug. "Yay! Love you, Wes!"

He smiled and shrugged me off. "Yeah, whatever, Hox, I said maybe!"

I wasn't too bothered about that though, because if I helped him get Barbie then he would be too happy to care what I say or do, and would definitely say yes to Jonah in our tent. A whole weekend of Jonah, his godly self just one compartment away. I was bouncing with excitement.

All I had to do was set up A Plan.

3

"*A*re you sure my hair looks OK?" Wes asked for the third time as we sat in our regular seats in registration, at the back of the class for blatantly obvious reasons, waiting for Mr Clumfield to start taking the register.

Mr Clumfield is a legend. We actually couldn't have a better form tutor. He's so funny – in his cracking Yorkshire accent he tells us a different joke every Monday morning that he learnt at the pub with his mates on the Friday before, to "make our start to the week that bit brighter"; and he has a proper dishy smile matched with deep, dark eyes, which makes me feel a little bit faint some days. He's also my English teacher, which is pretty cool, and just makes anyone feel welcome whenever. And he also shaved his (really hairy) legs for charity last year, and wore a skirt for the rest of the week. In the middle of November. Like I said, he's just a bit legendary in our school.

He was sat at his desk, with his own particular mug that says "CLUMMEISTER!" (God knows where he gets these things), scribbling away at some work or something. He furiously scratched something out with his pen and stood up suddenly with that full-of-fun grin and mischievous eyes.

"All right, guys, let's kick off your Monday. There are two muffins in an oven. One of the muffins says to the other muffin: 'Whoa, mate, it's hot in here!' – the other muffin screams and cries, 'Ahhh, a talking muffin!'"

I laughed, at least, along with the girls from my Blodge class, where instead of discussing plant and animal cells, we just sit and plan what we're going to wear Friday night. Faye Nichols and Jessi Townsend – they're those kind of girls who are pretty, intelligent and quiet, but like a good giggle. Amongst those laughing there were obviously the Mortimer twins, Maddie Adams and their crew of jokers. Maddie has one of those infectious laughs, and laughs at anything and everything – she's a right ray of sunshine on a cloudy day – and paired with Remi and Arno, the Mortimer twins, they could possibly form the most side-splitting trio known to man. The twins have a band called The Mechanicals, and they play locally for the youth club; not the best band in the world, but the boys know how to charm a crowd, and they help out at The Venue in town as roadies for the visiting bands there. It's pretty cool.

Then on the far side of the room the geeky girls, led by Verity Carter, who eagerly sit at the front (and who I know for a fact write 'I heart Mr Clum' in the backs of their homework diaries), went into fits of giggles too, but that was more to do with the fact that they fancy the pants off him than the hilariosity of his joke. Obviously, no giggles came from the tables nearest the doors — the kids like Henry Stags and Carly Lane who think they're hardcore because they listen to heavy-metal grunge and wear too much eyeliner — obviously they can't laugh because they're "making a statement" or whatever. I don't know exactly what the statement they are trying to make is, but if you can't crack a smile once in a while then I'm not sure if it's worth it.

Of course, Wes laughed too. Mr Clumfield is totally his idol. He stays behind some days to talk to him about Shakespeare, or novels, or obscure poetry that I've never actually heard of, ever. To be honest, English isn't really my forte — I'm more of a drawer than a describer — but Wes comes into his own there. He's a poet (but doesn't tell many people) and writes his own lyrics, and also does the tab to them on guitar. He's pretty good, actually; his lyrics are so fitting and his acoustic stuff is pretty much to die for. I wish I could write like that sometimes, but when I try to write everything gets a bit muddled up in my head, and doesn't go down on paper quite how I want it to; but Mr Clumfield helps a load, which is why he's probably my favourite teacher at Cathen.

"Is everybody feeling a bit lighter now?" he asked us, and we responded with a resounding "yes" as he picked up the sheet of paper from his desk.

Then someone knocked to come into the room, and Wes shot bolt upright again, hand going straight to his hair as he stared at the door. I swatted his hand down, and gave him a look that said

"Stop messing with it or I'll shave it off". Wes chewed his lip nervously. I grinned and gave him a wink: show time.

Oh, what laughs!

"Good!" Mr Clumfield continued, glancing at the sheet in his hand and striding over to the door. "This must be our newcomer to Cathen," he opened the door. "Hi . . . Emily, is it?"

I swear I heard every guy in the room's jaw drop to the floor. There she was: killer smile, hair like a shampoo advert, body of a model and the cheekbones of a pixie.

What a cow.

Naturally, I wasn't bitter at all, but smiled and waved as her eyes scanned the room and fell on mine. She instantly smiled wider and gave me a little wave back.

"Yeah," she said, turning back to Mr Clumfield and giving him a blast of her beauty. "That's me! Emily Drew, nice to meet you."

Mr Clumfield grinned at us all. "Hey, lads and ladies, we have a poet!" He turned back to Emily. "I'm Mr Clumfield, and I'll be your form tutor until you leave Cathen Comp. This is 10B," he said, gesturing to us lot. "They look a bit rough but they're all right really, and I'm sure they'll make you feel more than welcome! Take a seat."

Several of the boys, including James, Matt and Chris (those kind of guys who reckon they're real lady-killers) looked like they were willing to do a little bit more than make her welcome, so before she could get stuck sitting with them and being hit on for the rest of her life, I motioned for her to come and sit in the empty seat next to me that Wes and I had strategically placed there beforehand.

Emily replied with a warm "Thanks!" and made her way across

the classroom to come and sit with us, much to the Lady-Killer Squad's dismay.

"Hey, Wes . . ." she said, sitting down in the seat. I could practically hear Wes's mind screaming all kinds of elated, rudey words. Barbie smiled the Killer Smile. ". . . and . . . I'm sorry, I've forgotten your name!"

Smile, Holly; breathe in through the nose, out through the mouth. . .

My own smile threatened to break, and it was my own mind's turn to scream expletives. This girl was not good news. She was smiling at Wes and biting her lip in a bit of a wince because she couldn't remember my name. Apart from I bet she could. Playing up, making Wes feel special. Hmm. That's good for him, though. But she was all long legs and an evil mind: not the kind of girl a girl wants to befriend, now I was sure. More deep breaths. Think of Jonah. The tent. Jonah, his face, those eyes. . .

I was back on game.

"It's Holly, don't worry, and bless, it must be horrible trying to learn so many names so quickly!"

Oh, I'm so nice, you would almost think I was genuine.

She smiled and nodded. "Yeah, it's been really hard, my head's such a mess!"

"Yeah," chipped in Wes, with his voice smothered in concern. "It's hard moving places, I'm not surprised."

I internally raised my eyebrows. Wes has moved once in his life – from the smallest house on Millionaire's Row to the biggest. I'm sure the change was very painful for him, moving about thirty seconds down the street.

27

"It is," she grinned, not noticing that the class had broken into a frenzied whisper to discuss her arrival. Mr Clumfield had gone back to his desk, and was looking around the room to see who was present – his own way of doing the register: he feels it's more "foolproof" – but everyone else was stealing glances at her golden hair and bronzed skin. And most probably asking themselves why she was sat with us.

Wes and I aren't disliked, don't get me wrong – most people like Wes because he's funny and modest, with a sharp(ish) wit and cheery smile; and I am the Comic Book Kid, quite talented and lover of ice cream. We have a lot of acquaintances, but not many great friends. Unfortunately, our "closest" friends happen to be Margo and Finn, a.k.a. Stoney and Crony, who made their entrance at exactly nine a.m. – only fifteen minutes late, an improvement on last week's twenty.

When Margo enters a room, you know about it. She is one of those people who just gets attention everywhere she goes; she's just like a magnet for, well, all eyes really. Her PSG (Private School Girl – she *wishes!*) brunette flip of hair is always straight but voluminous; she always has perfect skin and teeth (due to the fact that she has every cosmetic available to man, because of "Mother") and would also be very pretty, if she didn't always look like she was sniffing creosote. And the model pout that so many girls attempt in the pictures on their web homepages? Margo has it. Times four. Maybe even five. It's fabulous, but matched with her "Darling, do *not* talk to me, for if you utter one syllable one shall staple your mouth shut" scowl, it's dangerous. But exactly like Mary and her little lamb; everywhere that Margo goes, Finn is sure to follow.

28

Henry Finn is a bit of a mystery. According to Cathen gossip, he's supposed to be one of my closest friends, but I honestly know no more about him now than I knew when I met him a year ago. He is still hidden underneath a mop of dark blond hair, iPod earphones in, and you're lucky if you get more than a "Yah, safe" out of him. I think he must talk to Margo, because they can't have had a relationship for about a year and not have talked to each other at all. But then again, if I were Margo's boyfriend, I don't know if I would talk; I suppose it would just be easier to agree and do whatever she wanted me to do. She's quite the little dictator.

Bang went the door, and in she stalked – Britain's Next Top Model. It was year ten "mock study leave" – studying in school, but not in school uniform – and so as usual, she took the rule to the extreme. In an intricately sewn summer dress, with a tiny blue beret perched on top of her voluminous mane, and eyes flashing, Margo shot a tiny smile at Mr Clumfield and drawled, "Good morning."

He is pretty much the only teacher she will smile at, if you can call the twitch of her mouth a smile. She just has a power that makes people do what she wants, without her batting a long, perfect eyelash. Finn floated into the room behind her like a shadow, all in black even though it was the height of summer, and shut the door silently.

"Yes, welcome, Margaret, Henry. Thank you for gracing us with your presence this morning. . ."

Margo waved her hand lazily in Mr Clumfield's direction, as if in acknowledgement of his comment, and looked over into our corner of the classroom. As her eyes clocked Barbie, I saw them flicker. Margo would be the deciding vote on whether Emily could come into our group, therefore deciding if it would be acceptable for Wes to, in his words, "woo her".

God, if you're listening? Help him.

What flickered in her eyes? Acceptance? No, couldn't be, not straight away. It took her a while to accept me, even though I am the Comic Book Kid and most people just accept that I'm an OK person, because my drawings are "well awesome, mate". So even though Barbie was gorgeous and obviously rich, pretty much right up Margo's street, it takes a long time for her to accept people, so that couldn't have happened yet. Margo doesn't please easily, as you may have guessed.

Disapproval? No, Barbie was a bit too perfect to disapprove of.

Amusement? Of course.

Margo likes nothing more than to cause a bit of mischief. She moved like a cat trained upon a mouse, and stopped at our table and clicked her tongue neatly, once.

"Here we go," muttered Wes under his breath to me.

"Darling, is this the girl you were nattering on about last night?"

She was talking to Wes, but her eyes were fixed firmly on the Plastic. If Barbie felt uncomfortable, she didn't show it. Or maybe it was just her all-American thick skin that protected her from Margo's unflinching gaze.

That's so like Margo, she doesn't do tact, and so poor Wes's face crashed into freefall for a millisecond, then pulled on the emergency cord and caught itself.

"Yeah, this is the girl we mentioned yesterday," he said, smiling at The Girl. "This is Emily." Margo's face was unreadable, but I knew something was going on in that head of hers. She may look like a doll, but I know that under that gorgeous mass of hair there is a brain that calculates quicker than, well, my calculator. Wes gestured to his twin almost apologetically. "This is my twin sister, Margo, and he's Henry Finn, mostly just known as Finn."

Finn brought up two chairs from the front with ease – he's much stronger than he looks – and set one down in front of Margo facing the front, then sat down in his own chair. He flicked back his hair slightly so we saw a glimpse of an eye (which is more than most people get).

Margo slithered into her chair sideways, still not taking her eyes from Emily, and rested her skinny elbow on the back of the chair, with her head in her hand. She pouted, looking like she was waiting for something.

"Hi, both of you!" Emily beamed. "How's it going? I just moved here from the US—"

"We gathered, dear," Margo cut in dryly. I could see a test forming in her eyes. "That is a rather large lifestyle change; why did you leave?"

"Oh, my mom got offered a job here, in the city, and Daddy works here a lot anyway, so it was pretty convenient," Emily smiled, thinly.

I felt another pang of sorrow for Emily, because she'd left a lot behind. It must be awful to move away from everything . . . then I looked down at her tanned legs and all of a sudden I didn't feel quite so sympathetic.

Margo didn't miss a beat and continued to talk in her brisk, emotionless manner. "Hardly convenient for you, dearest; you must be terribly lonely. Where are you living now?"

"Whittle Lane?"

Margo blinked. She wasn't really expecting that. Whittle Lane is not quite Millionaire's Row but it's the next rung down on the ladder. This girl had some serious cash. And cash is a very good friend of Margo Stone. "Its quite pretty, really," Emily continued, now almost aware of the test she was taking. "Not as big as my home back in the States, but how often would I use an outdoor swimming pool or tennis court out here in your unpredictable weather?!"

Touché.

After two years of seeing Margo intimidate and assess people, and having had her do it to me, I know when she's impressed. The slight eyebrow raise told me everything, and judging by the tiny exhale beside me, Wes thought so too. Margo clicked her tongue once more.

"Quite right, darling. Holly and dearest Wes will help you to settle in." Her eyes flicked to us for the first time. Wes smiled. "Welcome to Cathen."

Emily grinned at Margo, which is quite a brave thing to do, but it showed off all of her pearly whites to a T. Finn muttered something to Margo, who then nodded.

"Yes, quite right," she said to her boyfriend, then turned to Emily. "As you are so new in town, you must simply come to The Venue to hear a band play on Friday evening."

She smiled a wide, shark-like smile that was filled with a

mirth that couldn't quite reach her eyes, so her face remained cold.

I know that smile.

It's the smile of a plan hatching, a plan that will lead to mischief and mishap: the smile of a puppeteer ready to make her puppets dance.

Margo had just invited Emily to The Faeries' gig on Friday night. It's sold out, but Margo never needs a ticket in there; Remi lets her in on the sly, as he's fancied her since, like, year nine. And it's not like he's going to refuse Blondey Long-Legs here, so she'll get in. Emily looked at me for reassurance and I nodded, so Emily smiled and nodded.

"Yeah, sure, why not!"

"Oh, what fun!" Margo exclaimed, her face now a perfect mask of simple innocence. "And you should stop by the house next week! Why, you simply *must* come and meet Mummy!"

My stomach turned.

Meeting Mrs Stone?

Never fun.

4

We got off the bus and I smiled at the driver, who scowled back. Bus drivers can be mean. Very mean when you ask for a child return because you are actually under the child age limit, but the bus driver flat-out refuses to believe that you aren't older. This one had begrudgingly given me the child ticket, though, so he deserved the smile because I only had the right change for a child ticket anyway. Margo strode ahead of us with Finn a beat behind her, floating like a ghost. I could hear her drawl of complaint from ten metres; the chauffeur was stuck in traffic an hour away, so Margo had to get the bus back, like some "godforsaken plebeian". If I hadn't seen Margo cry once, I would have bet every penny in my bank account (that's six hundred and thirty four pennies, if you were wondering) that she was dead inside. Fair enough, she cried because her gold Gucci watch broke whilst we were all playing tennis, and she hit the ball with a bit too much fury – the ball went forward, the watch flew back – but it's still tears which show she must be a little bit human in there somewhere. Somewhere deep, deep down.

Because it wasn't my turn to pick up Lizzy, my little sister, we'd decided to go to Wes's. He and I ambled along to his house, keeping our distance from Margo's tirade, and he chatted on about the newest Wonder of the World – you guessed it, Emily Drew! – while all I could think about was if my hair had gone all fuzzy at the back, and why I'd worn the home-made denim skirt that I had fashioned out of an old pair of jeans last year. This morning I'd thought it looked good in the mirror, but now I felt a bit stupid. You just don't wear jeans to Wes's house. At least my legs are all toned from tennis season. Tennis is about the only sport I can do. I have to do some kind of exercise so all the ice cream doesn't come back to haunt my hips, so tennis is pretty convenient. However good my legs look, though, you just don't wear a denim skirt to the Stone household – coming to Wes's house is either the best thing in the world, or the worst: it depends on whether Mrs Stone is home.

We walked up the sweeping path that leads to Wes's three-storey mansion – I like to call it "The Palace", but only to my mum; if I said it to Wes he'd get a little bit huffy, like he always does when I mention the fact that he's got more money than Bill Gates. Well, maybe not that much, but pretty damn close. The path is so wide that two cars could fit down it, side by side, and it's covered with those little white pebbles that make everything look ... glossy. So, accompanied by the perfect crunching sound of the pebbles beneath our feet, the smell of freshly mown grass, the midsummer sun gracefully warming our skin, we arrived in front of the old brick house and up to the large black door with a white frame (notice that Wes's house is so perfect that it makes me burst into sensory description?! That's how awesome it is).

Margo had left the door open, so we wandered through into the magnificent entrance hall (you guessed it, complete with chandelier – I'm not making this stuff up!) to hear a tinkling laugh like silver bells, and the click click click of couture metal heels against a marble floor to see a tall, dark-haired, beautiful woman glide into the room, her expression a mirror image of her daughter's. Their faces matched to a T, even down to the dark, almost black, brown of their eyes. Wes's eyes are like that, all dark and mysterious, but also deep: deep, warm eyes that feel like they look right inside your head and know exactly what you're thinking. But the carbon copies Mummy and Daughter have threaten to pierce you so much sooner than invite you in.

So when Mrs Stone flicked her eyes over the pair of us, Margo bouncing in her wake with a flow of constant glossy chatter, like one of those tiny ridiculous dogs that rich poseur heiresses own as accessories. I definitely felt their icy black chill creep up from my sandal-clad toes all the way up my bare legs to my stupid denim skirt and high-street haltered top. But I like the way I look, I don't care – it's only when I step over that marble threshold into a house that could solve third-world debt if it was

36

sold and all the proceeds donated that I wish I were just like the heroine in my comics: equipped with the power of invisibility.

Wes turned to shut the door and Mrs Stone's clear ringing tones cut through Margo's stream of conversation.

"Why do you have to wear those terrible tatty jeans that drag so, darling?" A sharp intake of breath came from Wes as he clicked the grand door shut. He's a very cool and calm guy in everyday life, but the one thing that gets to him is his mother. He turned on his heel, clicking his tongue softly; the telltale sign for when Wes is trying to control his frustration. "I got you some delicious casual trousers from Ralph Lauren today; Juanita put them in your wardrobe."

As he started to walk over to where I was stood practically cowering in Mrs Stone's presence, his once-white Converse (which are now exclusively decorated with cartoons of Lameboy, H'y Girl and the members of The Faeries in cartoon form) squeaked on the polished floor. I could hear the sentence before she even said it.

"And what on earth are those on your feet? They look like a small child has scribbled all over them. . ." I could feel my face burn a little, and I looked down at my feet. My flip-flop-clad feet. My bare legs. My homemade denim skirt. Dammit.

"They're my shoes and I like them, Mother," Wes said through a forced smile, and he arrived by my side and I could feel the tension rise. "Just like how I like my jeans. And how I like the other things I wear, and the things I do."

I knew what was coming this time, too. It happens every time I come here and see his mother. Mrs Stone had been ignoring me just as steadily as Wes had been ignoring her mocking tones and I had been studying my shoes. She thinks that I am a bit useless, to be honest. There's no point in beating about the bush; it's true. My family lacks the cash that Mrs Stone seems to deem best above all other attributes in the world, like kindness or helpfulness, and Wes was about to address it. He was just waiting for one more remark from his mother, about how she doesn't think he presents himself like a Stone, or how he never does well enough or doesn't do his family name justice, and then he would throw me in her face. I sometimes think I'm his little bit of rebellion, his unconventional friend and a weapon against his mum, but I know I'm not really. He just gets angry because his mum is narrow minded and he's not, so he wants her to notice and accept me because "I'm a person too" or something. But I hate it when he does it, it's so awkward, so I just thought I'd interrupt beforehand.

"Wes," I murmured, still inspecting my self-done pedi. "Could we just go upstairs? Like, now?"

Wes looked away from his mother, then to my quiet, pleading expression, and then back to his mother in a moment of heightened unease.

"*We,*" he said pointedly, finally breaking the silence, "are going upstairs. If you need anything, just shout."

Wes strode to the sweeping marble (what a surprise!) staircase accompanied by the squeaks of his shoes, and I moved a few paces to follow, moving fast past Mrs Stone and not looking up.

Slap-clunk. Slap –

What was that –

– clunk.

Noise?

Slap-clunk.

Look down.

Pick up a foot.

Slap.

Put down a foot.

Clunk.

At that moment I vowed never to wear flip-flops again.

Slapsqueakclunksqueakslapsqueakclunksqueakslapsqueakclunk

I ran over to the staircase as Wes strode and between the two of us we made quite the crescendo. Way to make a dignified exit. . . Not.

Mrs Stone sighed, and raised her eyebrows just a fraction.

"So when will you dispose of those shoes then, darling?" she said, as if she hadn't heard his previous statements.

Wes took a deep breath and looked back at the Armani-covered witch.

"I'll chuck them when you start to admit that I don't want to be Abercrombie and/or Fitch, or when you start to acknowledge the friends that I've chosen. I'm not sure which will happen first, but to be honest, I'm not holding my breath."

I looked up at Mrs Stone, half expecting her face to turn to ice, her eyes to fire, and for harpy wings to sprout out of the back of her multi-thousand-pound suit jacket; but she just stood there with the lazy smile still in place, fixing her son with a level gaze.

39

"Show me when you try on the clothes," she ordered, once again as if she hadn't heard him. She continued on her way across the entrance hall over to the large oak study, her sophisticated heels making the delicate click-click-click once more, and Margo tottering in her wake with her "cat-got-the-cream" smile. In mid-stride, Mrs Stone finished her sentence. "And darling? When you walk, *do* pick up your feet."

"So its time for The Plan!" I exclaimed, after I had calmed Wes down with some ice cream from our emergency stash in the upstairs kitchen – otherwise known as the Spanish kitchen, by Margo and Finn, because it's Juanita's own personal kitchen that she can use for herself. It's small, but has a big fridge-freezer, which comes in handy for our secret stashes. In this house, ice cream is seen as evil (as it has more than two calories, so is obviously the work of demons) and so there isn't any in the family kitchen or larder. Juanita is more than aware of the rules, so when she goes shopping, we slip her a bit of cash and she gets us some in, and hides it in her kitchen in return for us lending her 90s boy/girl band CDs to improve her English. She's quite fond of singing "Spice Up Your Life" in the middle of making a curry, which always makes us smile. There is also a large tub of Ozzie's best chocolate ice cream (he calls it "SuperChocolate!") but that is for code one, dire, red-alert, ground-shaking disasters, like if Lizzy got taken to hospital, or if a Faeries gig got cancelled, or if we lost an iPod.

I'd managed to coax him into sitting on his bed with a spoon and tub whilst I had rummaged around his (rubbish tip of a) room for his iPod, plugged it into his (beast of a) docking station, and put on "Two Years" by The Faeries. It's about a boy who is stuck at home with his drunkard dad and a mum who couldn't care less, and how he can't wait to move out in two years' time – sample lyric: *I'll shout and scream myself hoarse/Just so you can hear/The point you always seem to miss/Only two more years of this/Our harmonious family bliss.*

OK, so his dad isn't a drunk, he's actually a really nice guy; a lot like Wes but with silvery hair, a posh accent and not a lot of spare time, because he's a surgeon at some big private hospital in London and spends most of his time there. But his mum really couldn't care less, so, for our economy-class Wes stuck in a business-class society where not one person listens to a word he says, the song's pretty fitting.

Soon enough, those sweet chord slides had soothed his mind, and I turned his thoughts on to other things. We had come round to the Palace to discuss a Matter of Great Importance.

"The gig!" I exclaimed, suddenly business-like. "That is going to be our first mode of attack."

I pulled out my folder from my bag and took out a clean sheet of paper from it, wrote "Plan BARBIE" in the middle, drew a circle around it and looked expectantly at Wes.

"Crikey, you are prepared, aren't you?" he said a little worriedly, and read the sheet. He raised his eyebrows. "Why 'Plan Barbie'?"

I tutted with impatience and rolled my eyes. "Keep up, Wezzer, it's code for 'Super-intricate and amazing plan to get

Wes the new all-American girl hottie called Emily Drew to be his super-cool girlfriend for ever and ever'. Duh!"

He laughed. "I don't want her 'for ever and ever', but yeah, I get the gist, you geek. So Friday, we have a plan?"

"Well, I have a plan that I'm giving to you. All you have to do is follow it and she'll come running, but it is important that you do not deviate from The Plan. Do you understand?"

Wes nodded solemnly. "Yes, ma'am. Completely. Tell me The Plan."

"Right. Margo has already unknowingly put into place Step One and Two of The Plan."

Wes looked a little surprised. "She did? When was that?"

"Today, when she asked Emily to the gig on Friday. That was Step Two. Step One was to make her part of our group." As I explained, I wrote it all down on the piece of paper like a giant spider-diagram I was told about in maths revision sessions. I've never used one before because I tend not to revise for trivial subjects such as maths, but it was actually pretty fun – I used colours and pictures for each Step in The Plan. I was really getting into it. "You see, if we make her a part of our group, then she will see us more often. If we see her more often, it is more opportunity for her to see you and how fantastic, amazing, funny and gorgeous you are—"

"You think I'm gorgeous?" Wes asked, eyes twinkling behind his glasses.

I suppose he's quite cute, in a way; nice eyes, good skin, great hair, nice smile – but it's Wes. I mean, *come on*, I don't look at him in that way. . .

42

"Nyeh, you'll do," I replied easily with a grin, as he poked me in the ribs. "But this week, you've got to be tip-top fitty, inside and out. This leads us to Step Three: finding out what she likes. I'll do some cunning girl-chat to find out what her type is, and we'll play up that side of your personality. We're going to pick out some stuff for you to wear for the rest of the week, and as I snoop and find out what she likes, we'll get you to emphasize that with your Wes-style. . .!"

"OK," smiled Wes. "So we get her into the group, we get her to come to the gig, we make me look good during the week . . . then what?"

My devious grin widened. "You get cosy at the gig, and prepare to ask her to come with us to Midsummer Rave, bay-bay."

"Are you sure that this will work?" Wes asked uncertainly, rereading my scribbled mish-mash of notes on The Plan. "It all sounds a bit simple."

"My darling boy," I purred, putting on my best Margo impression, "the course of true love always did run smooth."

Wes frowned.

"Erm, no, actually, Shakespeare begs to differ: 'The course of true love never did run smooth'."

Dammit. I said English has never been my strong point.

"Well, whatever. Shakey or no Shakey, The Plan will work and you will get your Barbie doll and I will get Jonah and it will be epic times all round. . ."

I grinned. Everything was about to fall into place, and I was falling into my favourite daydream: I'd get Wes fixed up with

Barbie, then I'd get Jonah to come share our tent, then we'd dance the weekend away, and then he'd turn around and say in a really husky and slightly Italian accent—

"Holly, bambino, you have-a always a-been the most bella girrl, the only girl for-a-me!" Wes exclaimed, stretching out his arm to me and laughing as his said it.

I had previously shared the Italian-sounding Jonah daydream with Wes, which was a big mistake, as now when I'm in the middle of a daydream he will start doing an awful impression of it, and I never finish my dishy daydream-fest. Annoying, stupid boy.

"Shut UP, you fool!" I cried with a huge smile as I berated him with a rather fluffy pillow, and he grabbed one too and started biffing me over the head with it.

"Aaah, NOOO, my *hair*! This means war!"

I rolled over and yanked another pillow off the bottom of his bed, then commando-rolled back with the duvet flying everywhere and tried to take him out from the knees, but he was too strong for my stupid weak, girlish arms and so managed to sit on top of me, strip me of all my pillows and hold one threateningly above his head with an evil smile plastered on his face, hair and glasses askew.

"Surrender?" he asked, raising an eyebrow.

"Never!" I cried, wiggling to get free, but shielding my eyes too in case of an unexpected biffing from Wes's pillow.

"All right," he sighed, shrugging his shoulders. "Your funeral."

At which he lifted the pillow high above his head and brought it down so I had to squeal:

"Noooo! No, I surrender, I surrender! Just don't pummel me PLEASE!"

He started to laugh. Putting the pillow down, he gave me his hands so we could stand up and pulled me up with him, but the duvet slipped under us on to the floor, everything went everywhere, and we ended up crashing back down on to the mattress, laughing like right loons and not breathing.

I was laughing so much that I cried, and started gasping for air. We sat up and he gave me a hug.

"Breathe or you'll pass out!" he laughed, and patted my back gently.

"Well, well, doesn't this just look cosy?"

We broke apart, me still breathing uneasily with a bright red face and both of us looking a bit of a mess. Ooop. I can see how this would look to an outsider.

"What?! Me and, and Wes?! No, no, no," I exclaimed in a gush of words, shaking my head and untangling myself from Wes. I know how she likes to stir things. "So not what you think!"

Margo raised an eyebrow.

"Dear, that was just a bit of soft mockery – but it seems that your defence mechanism is working right on the ticket. And what is this?"

She bent down with perfect grace and picked up The Plan. The Plan with four different colours, and glitter pen, and pictures . . . and "SECRET" written at the top (yeah, so I got a little carried away! I'm not sixteen yet, I'm still a kid!). When I had been making it, it had been a giggle, but now it was in her hands I felt a bit pathetic.

"'Plan Barbie'?" She looked up at Wes with a frown. "You like what you see in Emily? Isn't she a bit . . ." Margo flicked a look at me, and then back to Wes. ". . . far from your usual type?"

"*Girl* is his type," I replied, standing up to take The Plan out of her hands. I held mine out to her to receive the paper, but she wouldn't let go right away. Margo surveyed me closely with her big, cold eyes before letting it go; and as I walked back to the bed, she turned and stalked out from the room.

She waved her hand lazily behind her as she walked out the door. "Good luck, Winston. I daresay you'll need it."

5

"*H*olly, are you up yet?"

No, I am still asleep and trying to ignore you.

"Hols!"

I rolled over and snuggled deeper into my duvet, tugging it over my head so Mum became a muffled background sound. I didn't want to get up. I'd been having this amazing dream—

I was at this club, and the strobes had been going, and I'd been "throwing shapes in the Temple of Dance", as my dad calls it (normal people call it "dancing"), and suddenly The Faeries turned up and just started dancing with me! Chevans (drummer and charmer of the band) was looking me up and down, and kept winking; Vikki (the tiny blonde bassist, with all sorts of colours through her short hair) started to get her groove on with me, so we had a little shimmy; and then Matt (he's the gorgeous, moody lead guitarist who has a messy mop of curls and the best butt I've ever seen) started twirling me around, and I just couldn't stop laughing. It was so funny. In the strobe I couldn't see much and it was just so cool, I couldn't believe I was dancing with my idols, and then Matt twirled me around and around and around but I let go of his hand and flew straight into the arms of Robin Goodfellow, lead singer and bonafide, grade-A, lusher-than-lush super-star rock god. And he was getting closer, the strobes highlighting his gorgeous cheekbones and bright green eyes, and we inched closer and closer in slow motion for a perfect moment, I was so close—

And then my darling mother woke me up.

Drat.

But it had been a pretty spectacular dream, so I was still smiley when Mum came in, a towel wrapped around her wet hair, laden with clean washing wedged under one arm and the phone in the other. She shoved the phone into my face.

"It's your father."

Good morning to you too, Mother! I do hope you slept well. I grunted in thanks and picked up the phone.

"Morning, Dad," I mumbled, trying to find my voice.

"Hello, Berry! How are you this morning?"

He has always called me Berry, because I'm Holly, so I'm his little Berry, blah blah blah. It's nice, but no one else is allowed to call me it. It would just be wrong. Dad's voice was far too awake and cheerful for this time in the morning, but he had been up for a while because he's a postman. He works the night shift in the sorting warehouses, and then works the morning shift for delivery, so I don't see him loads, but he always rings first thing in the morning before I go to school.

Mum gracefully plonked the pile of clean washing on the bottom of my bed, picked her way over to my windows and, before I could stop her, threw open my curtains and pushed open my window in one movement.

"*Ahhh*, my eyes!"

"Did your mum open the curtains?" he chuckled.

"Don't stay in bed, as you'll be late! You need to get up — school won't wait!" Mum sing-songed on her way out of my room.

Ahh, too much activity for this early in the morning!

"It's not *that* early, it's eight o'clock!" Dad replied.

I didn't even realize I had said that aloud I was so tired; stupid school, starting so—

"Eight o'clock?!" I cried down the phone, suddenly quite awake. "Oh pants, I was supposed to be up *ages* ago, Wes is waiting for me!"

Dad laughed softly. "It's always a rush at the Hockers' household! Just tell me that you're happy, healthy and alive and I'll let you go."

"Happy? Yes. Healthy? Yes. Alive? Almost!" I shot out as I searched frantically for my hairbrush. I looked in my mirror and winced at my reflection: cat pyjamas and a strappy top, my hair like a bush and sleepy eyes? Ouch. "Are you OK, Dad?"

"Fit as a fiddle!" sang my dad. What is it with the rhyming and alliteration from my family so early in the morning?! It's what

49

comes with having young children, I swear; everything turns into a children's TV show. "The sun is shining, I am smiling and I'm most of the way through my shift, so I can't complain!"

I heard a clatter from somewhere below me and Lizzy gave an almighty wail. Mum's voice rang through the house:

"Hols, can you help me feed Liz? I need to do my hair – I've got a lesson at quarter past!"

Mum teaches extra English to some kids at school. She's got a new pupil starting today, but couldn't see them after school because she's got to take Liz to the dentist. They rearranged for this morning instead, I forgot. Damn! I'm going to have to text Wes and tell him to take the next step of The Plan without me.

"It all sounds a bit hectic there, love, so I'm going to let you get on. I'll see you later. Have a great day."

"Yeah, you too, Dad. Sorry! See you later, love you, bye!"

I chucked the phone on to my bedside table and jumped out of my squishy single bed, desperately trying to comb my hair.

"Yeah, Mum! Hang on a sec, I'm coming!"

I threw open my wardrobe and checked out its contents. Jeans, jeans, more jeans; shorts, skirts, leggings, jogging pants. . .

I took a look outside. Gorgeous sunshine, as far as the eye could see. Not one single cloud. Definite shorts day.

I pulled out a pair of shorts and my favourite T-shirt, shoved them on my bed, and ran down the steep stairs two at a time. At the bottom I took an immediate left, straight into the kitchen, where Mum was battling Lizzy into a high chair and a bowl of apple slices was all over the floor. Lizzy started shouting my name happily as she refused to go into the high

50

chair, and I quickly sprang into action; picked up the random bits of apple and shoved them into the bowl and rinsed them under the tap, then went and helped Mum with the high chair.

"Good morning, Liz-Biz!" I cooed, picking up my sister and giving her a hug.

"Hoh-wy!" she cried, her big blue eyes wide and blonde curls bouncing. She may look like an angel but I promise, an evil, evil spirit can live beneath that innocent exterior. "Hoh-wy, Hoh-wy, Hoh-wy! Mor-neen Hoh-wy! Brekky!"

"That's right, its brekky-time! It's time to sit in the big chair and eat some yum-yums!" I cried with more enthusiasm than I knew I had.

"Yay!" she squealed, and obediently let me pick her up and put her into the high chair.

"I've been trying to get her into that chair for ten minutes!" Mum exclaimed, exhausted. "She's always so good for you! How do you do it?"

I shrugged, passing Lizzy a bit of apple, which she started to gnaw on immediately. I *do* know why she's so good for me; I slip her a bit of ice cream every so often, which Mum won't do any more because she realized that it's bad for you. I tried to tell her that everything is bad for you nowadays, but she was having none of it. She says that giving Lizzy ice cream will "make her even more hyperactive than she is now", and she won't touch it herself because it will "stay on my hips for ever". But Mum doesn't need to know about our Secret Ice Cream Arrangement, so I shake my head and smile.

"I don't know. Maybe I have The Touch!"

51

Mum smiled. "Well, whatever you have, it's invaluable!"

I saw a glimmer of opportunity to address something I had wanted to address for a while. I knew it was a touchy subject in our household, but I just thought, seeing as the opportunity had arisen. . .

"Yeah," I agreed, nodding enthusiastically as I fed Liz a bit more apple. "Invaluable, that's interesting. I don't suppose . . . with me being *invaluable* and all, that I could have, well . . . I suppose you could think of it as, say, a *'summer bonus'*—"

"Holly," Mum's face went stony as she pushed the next load of dirty washing into the washing machine. The radio was blaring, Lizzy was singing some tuneless, unrecognizable song and chucking her piece of apple into the washing basket, and it was now ten past eight. Hmm. I was beginning to think that maybe I should have addressed this at some other, less stressful, time.

"Lizzy, *don't throw*!" Mum reprimanded and she picked out the apple from the socks. She looked up at me and sighed. "Look, I'm not going through this again. You know things are tight at the moment; your father is working himself into the ground and I'm trying my hardest to write the draft for my next piece *and* look after Liz. We're trying our best here. We just can't give you a huge allowance like some of your friends get." I knew that she was talking about Wes, but I blocked it out. "I can pay for your phone credit and give you a little bit of money each week, but that's it. So no *'summer bonuses'*, no sudden cash flows and no windfalls, hon." She looked up from her assault on the washing and looked me in the eye. I could see the strain in her face and the tiredness in her eyes, and the little bit of pain too. "I'm sorry, Hols." she murmured. "Just . . . not right now, OK?"

I nodded, feeling suddenly guilty. "Yeah, Mum. Don't worry, just thought I would ask!" Goodbye gorgeous bikini I was going to buy for MSR! I did an internal sigh, and then looked back at the clock and had a sudden shock back into reality.

"Ah! Mum, go get ready, your pupil will be here in a second!"

"Ahh, you're right! Thanks, Hol!"

And with that, she ran off up the stairs and I heard the hairdryer blaring a few seconds later. Lizzy started grappling for some more apple, so I gave her a piece and watched her eat it, her little eyes focused on it with such attention and her smile all cute and satisfied. She gave a little giggle and banged the apple into the top of the high chair, and then laughed, a proper little-girl laugh, like it was the funniest thing in the world.

If only I were so easily entertained.

Unfortunately, the things that entertain me are music, clothes and boys. All of which have to be bought, I thought bitterly; the first two with money, the third with good taste in the former coupled with good wit and humour, and most importantly with a great pair of—

The doorbell rang and made me jump so that I dropped the apple bowl again, but this time I cried out.

"Oh *dear*, Liz! Your apple went all over the floor! What a shame! It'll just have to go in the bin." I looked at the time: just after quarter past eight. I needed to get out of there and get going to meet Wes. I picked up the apple and chucked it into the compost out the back door. I made a sad face at Lizzy. "Brekky-time's over."

Lizzy pouted for a second, but then realized that it meant she could get out of the chair, so held out her arms to get lifted out. I picked her up as the doorbell rang again.

"All right, *all right*, *all right*, I'm coming!" I muttered, jogging through to the hall. I ran a hand through my now tamed hair and then opened the door.

To find Jonah Jones standing on my doorstep.

Jonah.

Jones.

My mum's new pupil was Jonah JONES?!

And he was there.

At my house.

Standing on my doorstep.

Looking at me like I was a Martian.

That was when I realized that I was still in my Kitty Kat pyjamas, with no make-up on, and with my baby sister banging me on the head with her last bit of mushed apple and crying out: "Bounc-ee, bounc-ee, bounce bounce BOUNCE!"

She wanted me to play the game where I bounce her up and down.

Great.

I wanted the ground to decide it was hungry for a bit of brekky too and just swallow me up right there and then, but it didn't.

"Hockers?" Jonah asked, his mind-melting eyes all quizzical and gorgeous. "What are you doing here? Am I at the right house?"

He took a step back to glance at the house number and I glanced sideways at the mirror. I had a bit of apple in my hair and my right eye was a little puffy. Oh, why do the bad things always happen to good people?!

"Errm. . ." I cleared my throat and just told myself to play it cool. "If you're here for English tuition, you're in the right place! Come in."

My voice miraculously sounded steady and friendly, as if I wasn't freaking out like crazy inside. Thank goodness. I stepped aside to let him in, and he walked into the house. He was wearing really nice dark jeans and a light polo shirt that showed off his arm and back muscles to perfection, and he smelt all clean and minty as he walked past. Oh be still my beating heart!

"I didn't know Mrs Cook was your mum," he started, as I shut the door. "Isn't your last name Hockers?"

I smiled. "Yeah, so is hers. She uses her maiden name when she teaches. Come into the dining room. . ."

Ahh, so awkward!

He followed me through and I gestured to the table as best I could with a scrambling child in my arms. He put down his bag and leaned against the table with a sexy smile.

"Sister?" he gestured.

I nodded apologetically. "Yep, this is Lizzy!"

"She's cute."

I shrugged. Ahh, I needed to get out of there! Quickly!

"Yeah, well . . . I better go get her dressed and, err . . ." I looked down at my pyjamas with dismay. ". . . get ready for school, too. . ."

Oh, how embarrassing.

I turned on my heel and started to leave the room as fast as possible.

"Wait—"

Hold the phone – did he just ask me to wait? For the second time in a week?

I turned around slowly, Lizzy still batting me on the head.

He was looking at his feet, and started to scuff his toe on the rug.

"Holly, I've been meaning to call you for the past few days. Well, I've been meaning to call you for the past few weeks, ever since. . ."

He trailed off dramatically, and I thought back to the night that we had kissed, in the corner of the room when The Mechanics were playing. The whole year was there. It was such a good night – I was wearing my new skirt and a really cute sparkly top so I felt really good, and then I was just dancing with Faye and Jess and up came Jonah, so I thought why not, I'll just dance with him. So we danced. And somehow we ended up in a dark corner in a lip lock, and he took my number! Talk about a Cloud Nine situation. He carried on talking.

"Because I'd really like it if we could do something, y'know . . . like," he looked up, chewing on his lip ring (hmm, lip ring) slightly. "This Friday . . . maybe?"

It took all my brainpower to stop my mouth from dropping open. There I was, standing in my messy dining room, in my pyjamas, wearing no make-up, with bits of apple in my hair and my little sister trying to beat me up – and the guy I'd been dreaming about for months asking me out.

56

To be honest?

This is so not how I envisioned this moment.

Silence filled the room and I realized that I had just let his question hang in the air like last week's washing.

"Because I kind of can't stop thinking about you. . ."

Jonah Jones can't stop thinking about who, sorry?

About ME!

"So . . . what do you think?"

I looked up at his expectant eyes and their power nearly knocked me over. What do I think? I think it sounds like heaven on earth, that's what I think!

"Sounds . . . good!" I managed to squeeze out. But then I remembered. "Oh no, I can't! I'm going to the gig on Friday. It's the Midsummer Rave bands setting up and doing taster acts, sorry."

Damn! My heart sank and I couldn't believe that the one night I got asked by the perfect boy to go out on a date was the one night I couldn't possibly go. Wes and I got our tickets for MSR as soon as they went on sale, but we decided to get the Maximum Tickets – the tickets that include passes to the actual MSR gig (and a camping space), but then also passes to the two warm-up gigs, one a week before MSR and the other the day before it started. It was so expensive, but Wes said that he would go halfsies with me, and the bit that he bought could be my Christmas AND birthday presents, and who can refuse a deal like that?! Anyway, the whole reason we were going to MSR was because The Faeries were playing their Best Set Ever with all of our favourite songs, but they weren't playing until the next week: the day-before gig and the actual MSR gig. The

57

gig that Friday was some other acts who had finished their tours and come to have a bit of a laugh and warm up the stage and hype for MSR. So because The Faeries weren't actually playing that week, I supposed I could just not go, but then I'd be letting down Wes, and he'd be gutted, and—

His smooth voice interrupted my jumbled thoughts.

"That's cool," he half-smiled. "I've got a ticket too. I thought you'd be going, so I got one and thought . . . maybe I could meet you there?"

YESSSS!

"Yeah." I smiled. Well, I pretty much beamed. "Yeah, that sounds good. I'll be there about half seven-ish."

"How about I meet you at the bar at the back, then?"

"Yeah!" I willed myself to say something other than "yeah". "Sounds like a rave, I guess."

"Cool," he smiled, giving me a wink. "I guess."

We stood there for a second, our eyes just . . . locked. Then my mum came rushing down the stairs.

"I'm sorry, I'm sorry I'm late!" she gasped as she walked into the room, carrying a copy of *Romeo and Juliet* and some help textbooks, rushing over to the table and setting it up. "Is it Josh?" she asked, eyebrows frowning in confusion.

He smiled and shook his head, his eyes still on mine. "No, it's Jonah, but no worries."

Behind Jonah, I saw Mum look up, look at me, then look at Jonah, and put two and two together that this is the boy I've been talking about for most of my teenage life. Her jaw dropped open.

Before she could say anything, I suddenly remembered that

58

I looked an absolute state and I was supposed to be meeting Wes in ten minutes.

"Er, I've got to go! I'll see you," I said, dropping my eyes straight to the floor as I felt my face flush, and I turned around to hear him say:

"Friday, seven-thirty, by the bar."

I rushed up the stairs, set Lizzy down on her bed, and changed her on autopilot. I couldn't believe it! I'd been asked out by Jonah Jones!

I put Liz in front of the TV to watch a quick round of *Teletubbies* (which is strictly forbidden by my cruel, Victorian mother, as it "melts children's minds"), tied my hair back and got the quickest shower in the world. I then practically jumped into my clothes, applied my make-up like it was an Olympic sport, grabbed my bag and ran down the stairs. The door to the dining room was closed, but it was enough to put the biggest smile on my face. I flew out of the door on wings made just for me, and grabbed my phone:

Recipient: The Best Friend
SORRY LAMEBOI RUNNING A
TAD LATE. U WILL NEVR
BELIEVE WAT JUST HAPND!
C U IN 5 :D
Send?

MESSAGE SENT.

I arrived at the gates five minutes later than planned, grinning like a loon. Wes was stood, leaning against a pillar, looking . . . pretty good, actually! We'd had a think the day before and I thought that if she was a Barbie, we should start off by dressing Wes as Ken. Actually, this is the Logic of Lizzy. I talk to her about a lot of stuff, and she usually just sits there and blinks, all covered in ice cream, and says the odd word like "Mams", "din-dins" or "Hoh-wy". However, this time she sat there, blinked, all covered in ice cream like usual, but then said "Barbie like Ken", and I thought it was worth a shot.

I saw that he was wearing the army pants we found at the back of his closet, some sandals (very manly-looking sandals – it took me ages to convince him that men's sandals are way more sophis than flip-flops) and a white T-shirt that showed off his permatan really well. Actually, the whole look gave a nice finish. And the tight top suited him – I never realized that he had such good shoulders before. He must have been doing some weights or something.

"Hey, handsome!" I called as I walked up beside him. "Don't you look good?" I winked.

He turned to smile at me self-consciously and tugged at the T-shirt. "Y'think? I personally feel a bit of a prat. Don't you think the T-shirt is a bit too tight?"

"Stand away from the gate and let me have a look at you."

I circled him to get a full vision of how he looked. No, the top didn't look too tight. It looked perfect. Like, really good. A bit wrinkled around his shoulders. I smoothed it out. Whoa, muscle! When did he get a bit on the muscular side? How did I not notice this?! I realized I was still stroking his shoulders. Whoops! I cleared my throat and took a step back.

"No, no, you look . . . really good!"

"Then why are you smiling all weird like that?" he asked suspiciously.

I checked back into reality and frowned.

"Smiling like what? I'm not smiling weirdly, *you're* smiling weirdly!"

Before either of us could figure out what I meant by that, I took his arm and steered him into the school gates.

"So. Are you ready, captain?"

He nodded, an "I'm-so-scared-that-I'm-going-to-look-an-idiot-but-yeah" nod. "Hmm. Suppose so." He looked at me sideways on,

61

and I was practically skipping down the pavement remembering Jonah's gorgeous half-smile when he asked me out this morning. He frowned, all confused. "All right, H – either tell me what's going on or quit jumping around. You're acting like a jelly bean and it's just a tad annoying."

I couldn't keep it in any longer.

I told him how Jonah had appeared at my door, and how I'd looked a right state, and how he'd talked to me, and how he'd been all shy when he asked me out—

"He looked *shy*?" Wes asked, nonplussed, pausing me in the tracks of my story.

"Yeah," I answered, stopping in my actual tracks and turning to face him. "Why do you sound so surprised?"

Wes looked uneasy. "Well, I just don't think he's the shy type. He's all masculine and . . . erm." He looked really uncomfortable and rubbed the back of his neck. "I don't know. . ."

He was really bothering me now. "What are you trying to say?"

"Well, I've always known Jonah to be the 'man's man' – y'know, like, the player?" he said gently. "So, I don't know, this could be, like, a thing to make you think he's really sensitive, because he knows it's what you like?" At the look on my face, he changed his tactics. "Well, I don't know. I suppose . . . just be careful that he's not going to play you, OK?"

I didn't know whether to be mad or not. Why was he trying to rain on my parade? Was he jealous? No, he couldn't be, not of me . . . And besides, he knew that I'd liked Jonah for ages and now he'd finally asked me out and it was perfect and—

OH, I got it! He was jealous because he wanted that for

himself! Just because I was getting my Mr Incredibly gorgeous (hmm, drooly drool drool) and he was a bit far off his own dream gal didn't mean that he had to go all protective big brother on me.

I decided to not be angry — I was in too good a mood and I didn't want to fall out with Wes just before the Best Summer Of All Time. Besides, I wanted Wes to be happy for me, and to have him be happy for me he needed Emily.

"Don't worry, Lameboy! I'm not going to let anyone play me, so no worries."

I gave him a big smile, and as we carried on walking into the school I shoved an iPod earphone into his left ear and switched on The Song.

"A bit of Faerie courage!" I whispered.

The guitar riff.

You're the riff that starts this story. . .

A bit of drums, and a touch of the cymbals—

You're the drums, your one song glory. . .

Which come in with the bass.

This song, your song, our song, it's true—

Then silence:

'Cause everything is idle when it's done for you.

Then the song starts.

A story about a boy who loves a girl (aren't they all?) and he loves her even though she seems like she doesn't even know, or care. It's one of those songs that comes on the radio and everyone who's anyone shouts "TURN IT UP!" It's called "Love in Idleness", and because it's A Bit Of A Tune, it's our theme tune.

So we cruised into school, cool as cucumbers, and walked into form just as the song finished. I put my iPod away and I pulled Wes back before we walked in.

"Just play it cool, boy," I whispered with a wink. "Be yourself for now. I'll find out her type today, and starting tomorrow we will make her yours!"

Wes took a deep breath and nodded. "OK, let's go!"

We walked into form, heads held high. Mr Clumfield wasn't at his desk yet, so we walked past it, saying hi to a few people as we went past, and sat in our usual corner. I turned to talk to Wes to clarify the plan one more time, but as I turned, Matt, Chris and James (the Lady-Killer Squad) surrounded us, looking at us intently.

"So," Matt said, eyebrows raised as he sat across from me. "We wanted to have a little chat with you."

"Yeah," added James, sitting down on Wes's right, nodding at him. "Yeah, just a small chat about a . . . a *thing*."

I shot Wes an ironic look. These boys think they're so subtle, but blind monkeys could see what they're talking about.

Chris sat down next to Matt. "Yeah, a *thing*. . ." He looked at Matt and lowered his voice. "You do mean *The Thing*, yeah? The thing we were talking about a minute ago?"

James rolled his eyes. "Yeah, *that* thing, Chris." He paused. "Matt?"

Matt took over. "So, the thing is, we are interested in something that has recently come into your possession." He cocked an eyebrow again. God, I was starting to feel like I was in some kind of really bad Mafia movie. "*Comprende*?"

Oh God, I *was* stuck in a bad Mafia movie. With a bunch of halfwits playing the Mafia. Any minute they'd be pulling out those porridge guns they use in *Bugsy Malone* and saying, "Well how you a-like-a me now, eh?!"

"Do you want to know about Emily?" I sighed, exasperated.

"Yeah!" Chris grinned, happy that I had caught on so quickly.

"Tell us: what's going on with her? What's the story? Is she single, like, fair game?"

"Or is she taken? If so, who's the guy, how big is he and could we take him?"

It was laughable. In fact, I did laugh. "All right, Hardy boys, take it easy! She's not like the Nobel Prize, y'know!"

They all looked at me, blankly.

"What?" Chris asked, eyes narrowed.

"Y'know . . . the Nobel Prize?"

More blank looks.

"The big prestigious award?"

They looked so confused that I didn't even know if their stupidity was funny any more. I tried a different tack.

"She's not a prize, y'know: a *prize* . . . something to be *won*. . .?"

"Ohh!"

"Right, yeah!"

"I get it. . ."

Finally!

"If she was *in* a game," Chris said, slowly, as if he was thinking hard. "She would definitely win." He hitched a big smile on to his face. "Because she's a PERFECT TEN!"

He held up his hands and received high fives off the other

...ike I was sinking in quicksand. I looked at Wes.

...d took the reins.

... – football!" he started, and all of their heads

...wards his, agog.

Typical boys.

"Here's the thing. This chick is single –"

"– all RIGHT!"

"– but she's pretty fly, right?"

"Yeeah!"

More high fives. Kill me.

"Right, well, it's like Man U and . . . and Cathen FC!" he said in a fit of inspiration. Wes doesn't watch football. "This girl? She's Man U! She's fit. She's athletic. She's worth a lot of money and she's got better legs than anyone else in the game, am I right?"

"You said it, boy!"

"Oh, yeah!"

"WOOP!"

"However," Wes paused, waiting for silence and clearly enjoying the attention. "You guys? You are a little bit more like the local Cathen. . ." He looked at the boys' expectant faces. "You're not quite up to scratch yet. You need a few more plays, some cash to buy some good players and your legs are in no way as good as hers. So if you ended up playing her? You would lose."

Wes leaned back in his chair, crossed his arms and cocked an eyebrow.

"*Comprende*?"

Matt looked from side to side at each of his friends; they both nodded, then Matt turned to Wes.

"We hear you, Wes, mate. You're so wise! She *is* Man U –" The boys nodded. "– and we are Cathen FC –" More nodding. "– but the Cathen motto isn't 'We like a challenge' for nothing, am I *right*?!"

James put both arms up in the air and did a sort of wolf howl, and the other two started chanting, "Cath FC, Cath FC, CATH FC! OI OI!" just as Emily stepped into the room. She caught my eye, waved, and headed over. She was wearing a little white, floaty skirt and a pink top, which I think I had as a kid for my Barbie. I waved back, and the boys turned around to see her coming over, and all suddenly reached for their hair. Matt flicked his fingers into a gun and winked, shooting an imaginary bullet at Wes.

"Hearing you loud and clear, my man," he said.

He jumped up and offered his seat to Emily, and the other boys leapt up too.

"Oh, thanks!" Emily said as she sat down, smiling.

They stood there like Charlie's Angel's for a second, and then Matt nodded to Matt.

"Catch you later, Wes."

Then he looked from me to Emily, and murmured in what he obviously thought was a sexy way:

"Lay-deez. . ."

He would have tipped his hat at us if he was wearing one.

Throughout the day, I kept on trying to catch Emily unawares; in English we had to work in pairs, so I asked her to go with me before anyone else could. We were working on *A Midsummer Night's Dream* by Shakespeare, and she was a little bit fascinated.

"So what, like, exactly happens in it? It looks a bit complicated."

"It is!" I pouted and she laughed. She really did have a cute laugh. Some people get all the luck. "So, OK. There are four regular Athenians: Helena, Hermia, Lysander and Demetrius; The Duke of Athens and the Queen of the Amazons, who are about to get married; Hermia's angry dad; a group of actors; and a bunch of fairies with their king and queen." Emily nodded. "Here's the dealio: in four days, the Duke is getting married. The actors are getting ready to perform at the wedding, but they are terrible and they provide most of the comedy in the play. The story that goes alongside that is of the four Athenians: Hermia's dad says that she has to marry Demetrius because he's handsome and rich —"

"— sounds like my kind of guy!" Emily exclaimed, grinning.

RESULT!

I carried on.

"— and he'd been promised Hermia. But she loves Lysander, and so they run off into the forest outside of Athens to get married, and they tell Helena of their cunning plan. Big mistake, because Helena is in love with Demetrius because they've already slept together – 'Ooer!', I know – and so Helena tells Demetrius and he runs after Lysander and Hermia into the forest, so Helena runs after Demetrius. Both lots of people, the actors and the Athenians, all end up the forest where the fairies are at play, and they mess everything up for everyone, but manage to put it all right again by the time the play ends!"

Emily nodded again. "You were right when you said it's complicated!" She looked back at her book and studied it intently.

"So what's your type, then?" I asked slyly. "Rich, gorgeous. . .? Anything else?"

She looked up from her book and grinned at me. "Erm . . . I guess . . . I guess he'd have to be tall! Tall and with dark hair?" I nodded encouragingly. This was exactly what we needed!

"Anything else?" I implored. "I like funny guys, guys that make me laugh?"

I was improvising, but she seemed to lap it up.

"Yeah, yeah, ditto! I like to laugh. But I don't know . . . what gets me every time is a bad boy."

Oh no. The one thing I was hoping she wouldn't say was 'bad boy'. Wes isn't really the bad boy type, is he?

"Hmm, yeah. I get you." I trailed off, enthusiasm lost.

"Like, *that* guy," Emily continued, gesturing out of the window next to us.

I followed where she was pointing to a guy walking up the front path, a guy wearing dark jeans and a light T-shirt—

"Jonah?!" My voice came out a little higher than I would have liked. I cleared my throat. Stay calm, Holly, take deep breaths. "Ahem, sorry; you mean Jonah?"

Emily looked back and nodded. "Yeah, he's so amped! I dropped a textbook yesterday and he picked it up for me. I said thanks for the help and he gave me this little smile – he has a lip ring, it's so hot! – and he said that he'd help me anytime."

I watched Jonah walk over the car park and frowned. Why was he being so helpful to Little Miss Perfect when he asked me out this morning?! As I watched him disappear around the corner, I decided he must have just been being really helpful

69

because she was new, and he might have seen her around with me. I mean, he said he couldn't stop thinking about me! Him offering his helpful services didn't mean anything apart from the fact that he was just a nice guy. He was sensitive – this morning proved that.

"Yeah, he's a nice guy like that." A thought hit me. "Yeah, actually, he's a really *nice* guy. Not so much of the bad boy, no – if you want a bad boy, you look to Wes."

Emily turned to me, frowning. "Wes?" she asked, looking over to where Wes was in deep conversation with Mr Canty and Mary Adams. Not the time to be looking a bit swotty, Wes dear! "Really?"

"Yeah," I nodded. Think fast THINK FAST! "Yeah, he lives up Millionaire's Row, y'know? And his dad had this old-school Mercedes, but one night Wes decided he was bored, so took it out for a spin."

"No way, shut up!" Emily exclaimed. "What happened?"

"He went speeding around the town, but then came home later because he had to meet his skater crew to go to some rave; he's always out at some rave or gig. . . Anyways, he put it away in the garage but then a few weeks later his dad got this hefty fine because the car had been caught on a couple of speed cameras, and Wes got grounded for months, but he just snuck out whenever he wanted, because he could."

Where on earth was this coming from?! I had no idea. OK, well, I did have an idea. The story was based on truth! His dad did have an old Merc, and one night in his rebellious stage, Wes was bored and did try to take it out for a spin, but he took off the hand brake and rolled to the bottom of the drive, not knowing what he was doing, and so crashed into a pillar. And he was grounded for months because the car was pretty damaged.

But that story makes him look even more of a wuss than normal, and besides, I was enjoying this story and Emily was lapping it up.

The Barbie was now looking at Wes with a kind of awe, like she was seeing him properly for the first time.

"Wow, I don't believe it! Wes a bad boy? I wouldn't have guessed it!" she exclaimed, and went back to her book.

"Yeah, who *would*?" I nodded, and went back to my book too. I needed to warn Wes about his shady past. Fast!

7

I filled Wes in, and we spent the next few days playing up his "bad self", as he liked to call it. We dressed him in darker colours, he wore skater shoes, I made his hair a little bit messier — I even tried to get him to wear contacts, but he just flat-out refused, drew the line at that. He hates putting his fingers in his eyes.

"Oh, don't be such a wuss! Look, I'll even do it for you. . ."

I practically straddled him with contacts in one hand and solution in the other whilst he cried out, "No! No, no, NO! I'd sooner let you . . . *pierce my ear* than stick your fingers in my eye!"

I paused as he struggled underneath me and thought about Jonah's lip ring (hmm, lip ring). Jonah's a bad boy. It wasn't a bad idea.

72

So that was how ten minutes later, Wes was sat with a bag of frozen peas stuck to the side of his head (we couldn't find any ice), and me sat on the bed next to him with an apple, sterilizing a needle with a match and some TCP.

"Done!" I murmured, wiping the needle once more with TCP and then setting it down on the sterilized tissue on his bedspread.

Wes looked at me with a disgruntled expression, peas still on his ear.

"I have a headache," he explained, taking the peas away. "Why do I let you talk me into these things. . .?"

I grinned. "Because you know that I'm always right. And because this time, if I'm right, you're going to look really, really hot!"

He looked like he was going to be sick.

"OK. So are you going to give me something for the pain, Nurse Hockers?"

I hadn't thought of that. I pulled up my school bag.

"Errm, I could give you some paracetamol?" I said, rummaging around. "Ooh! You could bite on this, too!"

I gave him my pencil.

"I think I'd rather have the drugs. . ." he said, reaching for them and taking two.

I took a deep breath.

"OK, let's do this! Lie down."

"And you're sure you know how to do this?" he asked me as he leaned backwards on to his pillow.

"Yeah, sure!"

I wasn't about to tell him that I'd never actually seen it done in real life, or done it myself, but instead was basing all of my piercing knowledge on *The Parent Trap* where Lindsay Lohan pierces her twin's ears, even though it wasn't her twin because she doesn't have one, it was just Lindsay again. I have no idea how it was made, so that film blows my mind every time!

So I sliced a bit of apple off, shoved it behind his ear, and got my needle ready.

"Got the needle, got the earring, everything is sterilized, we're good to go!"

I leaned forward. Now was not the time to start feeling a bit sick. I put the needle to the dot we had drawn on his ear.

"OK, do you trust me?"

"What?!" he cried incredulously. "What are you doing to me? Of course I trust you, I don't trust anyone else! Just do it before I change my mind!"

I nodded and cleared my throat.

"On second thought," he muttered. "Could I have the pencil, please?"

I gave him the pencil with shaking hands.

"Wait a second – are your hands *shaking*?"

"Nope. On the count of three. One, two—"

"AHHH! YOU SAID 'THE COUNT OF THREE' YOU—"

The needle was through and I thought I was going to be sick. Never, *ever* again.

I backed off.

"Holly, what are you doing?" he yelped. "You've still got to put the earring in!"

I took a deep breath and went back to his side. He had bitten through the pencil. Yikes!

"Are you sure you want me to do this? I mean, I could just take the needle and bandage it right up if you wanted!"

He shook his head and scrunched his eyes. "Just do it. Now."

So I did, and after a second go I pierced his ear. Then I pretty much collapsed by his side as he admired the ear in the mirror.

"It's good," he whispered, smiling shakily. "It looks pretty good!"

He sat back down on the bed and pulled me on to his knee, giving me a big bear-hug squeeze.

"Thanks, H'y baby." He grinned happily, looking into the mirror in front of us. The earring glinted back. He looked at me in the mirror and laughed. "I can't believe you did that!"

I watched him laugh off the tension of the previous few minutes, and then looked at my own reflection. I was white as a sheet.

"Yeah," I replied humourlessly. "No worries. . .!"

I felt like I was going to faint.

It got to Friday. Friday night was gig night.

I'd been flying around at home after I'd got back from school – I had no idea what I had been thinking! I'd been so busy trying to sort out Wes that I'd forgotten about planning for tonight.

The past couple of days had gone quite well. Wes was actually suited to the darker side of life, and his charming wit was in the zone. But I had caught him holding the door open for Emily the day before, to which I'd shaken my head profusely. In horror, he just let go of the door, but it swung back and hit her in the face, leaving a small bruise. Not what I was going for, but she saw the funny side (crazy, always-happy American girl). Apart from that small glitch, Wes's makeover had become a success. He'd even managed to get her number, and they had been texting a bit—

"But don't text her too much," I had warned him. "Because half the attraction in bad boys is that they are aloof".

"A-what?"

"Aloof. Y'know, like, mysterious."

"Ooh, right."

I hadn't seen his texts, but I hoped to God they weren't over-the-top vague or "aloof", or else she might just have thought that he was an astonishingly dim person and backed off like he had the plague.

So on Friday night after school I'd got home, chucked on a face pack and The Faeries' first album (*Ill Met By Moonlight*), ran myself a bath and opened my wardrobe – and felt like Mother Hubbard. Seriously, talk about bare cupboards?

"Mum!" I shouted, biting my nails. "Mum, could I go through your wardrobe?"

She popped her head around my door.

"Oh sorry, I didn't realize you were upstairs—"

"Holly Marie Hockers!" she exclaimed. "Your room is—"

"Mum!"

I rolled my eyes. She was looking around my total box of a room, and it was completely covered in clothes. Not kidding, I'm talking all of my clothes – *everywhere*. You couldn't see my

76

carpet, you couldn't see my tiny single bed, you couldn't see my bedside table; the only thing you could see was the walls, but really you couldn't even see them because they were covered in pictures of The Faeries. OK, my room was a bit of a tip. So what?! Didn't she know this was possibly the most important night of my life, and so this was so blatantly *not* the time!

I took a deep breath, put down the cute netted skirt I had been holding, and pressed my hands together dramatically.

"Do you remember what tonight is?"

It was like the final question on University Challenge. Mum never remembers anything that I've got going on, and so when I ask her a question like that she always squints and thinks really hard like her whole future depends on it. Usually I think it's funny and bless her rubbish little memory, but this wasn't a laughing matter.

Finally, she took a stab in the dark.

"You're . . . going out?"

I nodded with wide eyes.

"You're going out . . . to a gig?"

I nodded faster.

"You're going out . . . to a gig . . . with. . ." Then her mouth dropped and she squealed. "Ooooh, I remember, you're going out with *Jonah*!"

And the winner is. . .!

"Yeah!" I squealed back, the excitement filling me up — but then I looked back at my room filled with clothes, none of which I could wear, and the dread deflated my bubble. "But I have nothing to wear! Nothing, nothing, nothing!"

Mum pushed the door open (with a struggle) and came and sat on my bed.

"Hol, you've got more clothes than me, Liz and your dad put together. How can you have nothing to wear?"

I pouted.

"I know I have clothes, I just need something different! I have to look good tonight. But not just good, like – super good. Amazing! So drop dead gorgeous that I sparkle and shine like some Christmas fairy and light up the floor. But maybe not so festive, because if I turn up looking like a Christmas tree I'm pretty sure I'll get jumped, or laughed at, or—"

"Stop! Take a deep breath, you're rambling."

I took a few deep breaths whilst she continued.

"What were you thinking about wearing?"

I looked around my room.

"I don't know. . . A skirt, 'cause it will be hot inside? Or some tight jeans? Or . . . oh, I don't know!"

I collapsed into my pile of clothes, panicking.

"Right!" Mum declared, picking up the clothes off my bed. "You're going to go get in your bath, take off that face mask because you look like Frankenstein's bride –" I touched my face and looked in the mirror. I did look a bit dead with the grey mask on. "– and I am going to pick you out something to wear!"

Hmm.

"Erm. . ."

"It's OK!" Mum exclaimed. "I'll fix it, you'll see! You'll look hip!"

Oh dear. I was a little bit worried, but she practically ushered me into the bathroom and shut the door on my stuttering face. So I just gave up, got in the bath and listened to my iPod.

You make me feel seasick
Because you're so unpredictable
One day you're on my side
But the next you've swam out with the first tide
With all of my pride and confidence.
I just can't keep up the pretence
That you and me are meant to be
Because:
You're just the thorn
In my side.

I got out of the bath feeling good, and took my iPod back to my room, which was tidy (wahey!) with some clothes on my bed.

I walked up and found my new tight jeans, all washed and ironed so they would make my bum look good (RESULT!) and a T-shirt.

It was black, with frayed short sleeves and front ripped diagonally across the top of the chest. It was really hot. I picked it up, but something was weird on the back. I turned it over and saw that the back was sliced horizontally four times, so that it would hang off my back a bit.

It was really, really, *really* hot.

I dried my hair double-time, curled it and then pulled on my jeans. I looked at the top on my bed. Where on earth had Mum got it from?! I made a mental note to tell her that she was my favourite mummy and that I would love her for ever for this amazing act of . . . amazingness! I pulled it over my head and admired myself in the mirror. Oh my God, I looked awesome! I was going to kill at the gig.

I was really tempted to take a picture and send it to Jonah, but Wes rang.

"Hey babe, guess what? I'm wearing the best shirt ever!" I exclaimed, still admiring myself in the mirror. "It's soo awesome!"

"Erm, good for you. . .?" he replied. Huh, boys! They don't get excited like girls do. I'd have to ring Jessi later and tell her, she'd get excited. "Look, I was ringing because we've got a slight situation with The Plan."

The Plan was that Wes, Emily and I would all meet outside The Venue at seven-fifteen. Well, that's what Emily thought the plan was. The more detailed plan was that Wes would text Emily and ask her to walk with him, then stop by Emily's at seven, so that they could spend a bit of impromptu time alone. Genius!

"Why, what's up? Is Emily not walking with you?"

"Yeah, she is," he said quickly. "That part of the plan is going OK. She said we could walk together, so we'll be seeing you there."

"Oh, that's good!" I exclaimed, but then panicked. "So what's wrong? Is Margo not getting her in any more?"

"No, she is," he murmured, a bite to his tone. "Margo disappeared a while ago. She's probably gone to make some kids cry somewhere," he muttered darkly. "The problem is that before she went, she told The Mother that I 'have a date' with Emily. She just loves to stir that pot; she knew it would wind me up – she knows I hate Mum knowing my business. Anyway, The Mother apparently found out that Emily was the newest money in town, and was so happy that I seemed to be taking a interest in someone 'right for me' that she said –" Wes put on his best "Mummy" accent. "– 'Dear, you simply must bring her home, I'd love to meet her, she sounds just darling!'"

"Ohmigod!"

Disaster!

"But your mum . . . she's . . . she's. . ." What was the best way I could put this? "She's scary!" I blurted out. "And a little bit crazy! She can't meet her, she actually can't, she'll scare her off and then the entire plan will fall to pieces!"

Possibly not the best attack, but never mind. Margo always just wants to mix everything up – she loves nothing more than to make trouble for everyone else and then to watch the chips fall. I decided to re-jiggle The Plan.

"Look," I said, suddenly assertive. "We just need to get through tonight and then regroup. What are you up to tomorrow?"

Wes paused, thinking. "Nothing – I'm not doing anything, but aren't you covering a shift for Ozzie?"

Damn.

"Yeah, I am. Humph! Right – tomorrow night?"

"My mum's not in – she's at a dinner, so you want to come round here?"

"Perfect!" I grinned. "I'll bring us a supply from Ozzie's and we can fix it, no problems. But back to tonight, are you wearing what we said?"

"You bet."

81

The doorbell rang, and my mum shouted up.

"Holly, it's for you!"

I gasped. What if it was Jonah?

"Look, I've got to go," I whispered. "I'll see you later!"

"Yeah, all right, see—"

"Thanks, Mum!"

I put down the phone and chucked it on to my dresser, then checked my reflection. No make-up. Yikes! At least my hair looked good. And the top really was killer. I didn't even hear the door open.

"Darling, I do rather like your shirt. Very *Project Runway* meets . . . Goth. Truly a daring number indeed – so unlike your usual, ah, *style*."

I turned around to see Margo dressed to kill in the best LBD (Little Black Dress) you have ever seen (think Audrey Hepburn in *Breakfast at Tiffany's*, but short). She looked stunning, as ever. You would think she was going to have high tea in a Parisian black-and-white art movie, not going to see a band. But that's Margo for you – always doing the unexpected.

Like turning up at my house, unexpected and alone.

I could smell a Chanel-covered rat.

"Erm, thanks," I replied cautiously. "Nice dress. What's up?"

She prowled into the room, over to my dresser, where pictures of Wes and me were stuck inside the rim of my mirror, along with a picture of my mum and dad, and then a picture of Lizzy and me. There were three pictures of Wes and me. One from last summer, where we were sunbathing and decided to put lines across our cheeks in sun cream like we were Native

Americans; we're both cross-eyed. Then there's one from his birthday last year where everyone had to dress up as little kids – me in huge denim dungarees with bunches and drawn-on freckles, and Wes dressed up as Dennis the Menace. The last one was the most recent. Mum took it whilst we were just messing around in the back garden a few weeks before, and I'd stepped on some glass down the bottom of the garden (probably a bit that I hadn't managed to pick up after my last party that the folks will never, *ever* know about) and cut my foot. Mum had been taking pictures of Lizzy out in the garden in her sun hat, to send to my aunt. Wes had insisted on carrying me back up to the house, and Mum had just taken the picture: we were both in hysterics, I had my arms wrapped tight around his neck and was looking up at him, grinning like a loon, and our faces were inches apart but he was looking back at me, laughing and staggering like he was going to fall over. I love that picture. It's so happy. Mum put it in black and white, so it's all arty, too. It looks like one of those pictures you find already in the picture frame when you buy it. I look pretty in it – my hair looks all shiny and soft – so I've put it up with the others.

Margo went over and picked it out of the mirror, looking at it as she talked to me.

"Dear Winston is taking Emily to The Venue tonight, is he not?"

"Yeah. So what?"

"Hmm. The two of you usually do this kind of thing together, do you not? But instead Emily is going with my brother?" she drawled, putting the photo back in its place.

"Yeah," I started defensively. "Because he likes Emily, and I've got Jonah."

She moved her head to the side on a tilt.

"Jonah?" she asked, as if uninterested. "Jones?"

"Yeah," I said again, but this time defiantly. "Jonah Jones. I'm meeting him tonight."

"Are you? Emily is going with Winston, and Jonah with you. And you will all meet up together at some point in the duration of the evening?"

I nodded.

"Now that is interesting," she cooed, surveying me with her unfathomable eyes.

"And why would that be interesting?"

She was beginning to get to me. There was something in her eyes, a dark twinkling. Then it was gone.

"No reason at all, darling, of course!" She moved to my door, and was just about to leave.

"And darling, don't fret when you bump into Emily and Wes, and she and Jonah are so familiar with one another. They should know each other quite well by now, I expect. After all, they have been texting back and forth all week! Have a lovely evening, Holly, dear."

8

*H*ow was I expected to have the best night of my life after that?!

Margo left and I sat down heavily on my bed and thought hard.

Emily liked Jonah – she said so in English the other day. Jonah liked Emily, platonically at least, because he offered help to her "anytime" when he picked up her books. They'd been texting. Jonah hadn't texted me. But he had come around to my house, which was better than a text. And he had asked *me* out.

After looking at the evidence, I came to the conclusion that I was the one who Jonah was meeting at half past seven at the bar, not the long-legged bimbo. And besides, she'd been texting Wes too. So she must like him. And after the gig, she would know that Jonah was interested in me, not her, and so everything would be all right. Margo just couldn't keep herself to herself; she could never just let things lie.

Well, not this time.

I chucked on another CD and put on my make-up, dancing around the room and singing into my hairbrush. Tonight was going to be just that little bit awesome, I was going to dance like crazy and no one was going to ruin it!

I walked, because it was a perfect summer night, warm without being sticky. The moon was out already, with the sunset starting to take place, so the air seemed sort of magical. As I strolled along, I got the feeling that anything could happen – Mum would have said it was a night when pixies come out and play: a night for romance and mischief.

I got to The Venue a few minutes early, and walked up to the queue already forming outside. Teenagers from Cathen and surrounding villages and towns were in the queue; I knew a few who like the music scene around here and who I bump into frequently at gigs I go to. I love The Venue building. It's big and black, with posters all over the walls where windows should be – posters of all the bands that have played there, posters from the Midsummer Raves before this one, and on the door was a massive poster advertising this year's MSR, with a list of all the bands playing down the right-hand side. Halfway down in big black letters was "THE FAERIES". I felt a thrill of excitement down my spine. Next week they would be on this stage! In seven days I would be, like, metres away from Robin. My heroes close enough to touch! The thought was like a blaze of fire running through me, making me feel indestructible and red hot. THE VENUE was written in thin silver letters above the door, tarnished like they had never been looked after.

The thing about The Venue, though, isn't the look. It isn't the posters, or the impressive list of names on the outside, or the friendly, rock-star-dressed staff – it's the atmosphere. The Venue just sort of calls you in: it just feels alive. On band nights the bass calls to you from deep inside, like the heartbeat of some giant melodic monster sleeping on the pavement. You can feel it as you walk past: its heartbeat calling yours to come and dance and rave and just beat in time with it. It really does take your breath away. Coming here is like a drug that leaves you on an unbeatable high, so I make a point of coming here and overdosing at least once a week.

I arrived at the front of the queue, waiting where I said I would meet Wes. No one was allowed in yet, so the doormen weren't busy. Well, I say doormen – more like door boys.

The taller of the two spoke into his radio.

"Salut? *Salut!* OI TK! You plonker – *oui, c'est Remi!* – ask Len if we can let 'em in yet, over."

Remi is the only person in Cathen who talks like that. A sweet French accent from his mother, and then a harsh British one following it, from his friends – he's so strange, but awesome. I've been friends with the twins pretty much for ever, because we used to play together when we were tiny and we all grew up in the same town, went to the same primary school and then to the same secondary school, and are now in the same form.

We're all into the same kind of music so we used to come to The Venue together a lot. Then their band (The Mechanicals) picked up and they started playing here, I used to come and watch. They're pretty good, and they play with some of the other local acts, which is fun. They took part in the Cathen Battle of The Bands last year and won, so they're doing pretty well! And because they play here, they managed to swipe themselves jobs!

It's so not fair; it's like the dream place to work for your average Cathen teenager. OK, so the twins are the doormen, they wipe up spillages, they clean the whole place afterwards, but still — they work at The Venue! It's skivvy work but it's more than worth it. The reason everyone wants to work here is because it means that they get free tickets to *everything* (yes, even MSR) and they get to go *backstage* and — this is the best part — they MEET THE BANDS. That's right — in a week's time, they would meet The Faeries! I would clean up a thousand spillages if it meant I could meet them. Remi and Arno are so lucky!

But it's also a perk having them as your friends — it means that you can jump the queue a bit, and you get a heads up on what tickets are coming on sale. So it's pretty good to have friends in the business.

"Hey, boys!" I called over the metal fence. "How's tricks?"

Both blond-headed boys turned around, grinned and walked over to me.

"Not bad, Comic Book Kid, not bad at all," Remi replied, looking me up and down. "You've scrubbed up a bit, haven't you? You're not offending my eyes as much tonight as you usually do!"

"Yeah, what's the occasion?" asked Arno. "You don't have to get dressed up to see us, you know that."

I laughed and smiled. "Tonight's no ordinary night, gentlemen," I proclaimed. "I have to look a little bit kick-ass."

"Mission accomplished!" Arno said with a cheeky wink. "So who's the bloke?"

"Must be a blind date," Remi stage-whispered, whilst still looking at me. "Else if he knew what she looked like, why would he come out with Hockers?"

Arno laughed. "Maybe it's got something to do with her knoc—"

"*Actually*," I interrupted, leaning on the gate and trying to look serious. "It's neither a blind date nor anything to do with my, *ahem*, looks. We've got common interests."

"Each other's tonsils?" supplied Remi.

"Jumping around in the dark, surrounded by lots of other people?" guessed Arno.

"No!" I couldn't stop myself from laughing this time. These boys just don't let you take things seriously. "*Music*, blates!"

They looked disappointed.

Arno's radio crackled and he turned around to answer it.

"So," Remi smiled, running a hand through his hair, trying to be light and offhand. "Is Margo coming tonight?"

Oh, he's *so* sweet. Margo isn't right for him because she's way too mean and he's just so nice, but it doesn't stop him being completely head-over-heels gaga for her. She's like this goddess to him, and when she's around no one else gets a look in. The sad thing is she knows that he wants her, and she uses it to

89

her advantage. Talk about manipulative, jeez! I thought back to my room, Wes telling me that she had told his mother, then her trying to mess up my head about Jonah – the thought of her made me bristle.

"Hmm, I think so." I nodded coolly, but Remi didn't seem to sense the tone, and rambled on enthusiastically.

"Because she texted me before, asking if I could put Emily on the list, so I did, and then I texted her back asking if she was coming, and if she wanted putting on the list, and that I hoped that she was coming – but she didn't text back."

Oh, poor naïve Remi!

I wanted to tell him that he was wasting his time on Margo because she was just using him for tickets, but I didn't have the heart.

"I wouldn't wait for her, Remi," I smiled pointedly.

"Oh I won't," he said unconvincingly. "It's just that I need to be here to let her in when she gets here, because she says that it's always nice to see me. And her smile is so amazing, and she's so happy when I let her in for free that—"

He paused mid-sentence. I raised my eyebrows, hoping he got the subtext.

Remi continued quickly, "I'll go inside soon anyway, because The Dandys are on first and I don't want to miss their set. . ."

Of course he didn't get the subtext. Boys never get the subtext.

His voice trailed off because he saw Wes turn the corner, accompanied by the longest pair of legs I've ever seen, and the shortest pair of shorts. Maybe I should have briefed Emily on gig wear before we came.

Arno turned around.

"*Mon frère*, we can start—"

The words turned to mush in his mouth as Emily and Wes approached. Wes looked like he was telling a story, and Emily was listening intently, and when he told the punchline she giggled, and leant on his shoulder. I couldn't help a twinge of anger above my stomach. She'd been texting Jonah.

"Great *scott*, that girl's hot!"

"You can both shut your mouths now!" I hissed, and the Mortimer twins instantly closed them.

"Arr, *no*!" Wes shouted. All the boys in our year do that to Arno – they think they're being witty. "And Remster, my favourite front man. How's it going?"

"Hey, you guys!" Emily exclaimed as she walked up, greeting the boys. They nodded in reply. I smiled at Wes, who grinned and winked back. Emily's sea-coloured eyes fell on mine. "Hey, Hols, how's it going? I've just been hearing some stories about you!"

I could feel my cheeks burn a little. Why was he talking about me? He should be getting to know *her*!

"Oh yeah?" I said, trying to smile but just ending up with some sort of grimace, glaring at Wes. "Nothing too gruesome, I hope. . .!"

"Hey, Rem, it's time to let people in now," Arno said, still staring at Emily.

"Yeah, let people in. . ." Remi echoed, also still looking at Emily. Then it clicked. "OH, let people *in*, right, yeah! Come on then, Hols, Wes-man and Emileg – I mean, Emily!"

91

We went around the side and scooched into the entrance, the angry glares of the people at the front of the queue digging into our backs as we did so. The familiar scent of the place set me at ease straight away, the dark walls and wooden floor swallowing me up and making me part of it. The place had serious vibes. We went straight past the locker room through to the narrow stairs, and as I climbed them I could almost hear the footsteps of the legends that had taken those stairs before me. Before I knew it, I had pushed open the black double doors and stepped into the room.

It was like a church, but with a much lower ceiling and no pews: a long rectangle that led up to the altar (the altar obviously being the stage). The same rule applied to both places, too: you came here to worship. To the left, the bar was gleaming — lit up on the inside with dark red lights, the bar boys from the sixth form mooching around, waiting to be asked to serve. The doors were on the back of the room, where the wall curved "for acoustics" I was told. This curved back wall was covered in graffiti: bright and bold letters spelled out "The Venue Presents", outlines in glow paint, and then hundreds of signatures of bands underneath. I wasn't lying — this was the magical place of legends and heroes alike.

And I only lived ten minutes away.

There was already a lot of activity going on: roadies were carrying equipment around the stage, microphones had been placed, people were walking across the floor to the bar and going through doors to fetch things; some people were also stood down in the pit next to the stage. A metal fence that came up to just under my shoulder separated the pit from the stage, so that the bands couldn't get mauled by over-excited fans. The norm for me was to get to the front with Wes, to "the cage", as we called it, and hang on to it for dear life for the night. It's the best place to be because it's right in front of the bands. You do get crushed, because there's a surging crowd behind you and they are squishing you into a metal pole, but it's worth it. Sometimes I think I'm a bit of a music junkie, and I need to feel the music and have it blasting in my ears to feel secure, but Wes says he feels the same, so at least I'm not alone. It's why we love gigging it so much – the atmosphere and the feeling you get, and sharing it with someone – it's unreal. The only thing that could be better than being right at the front of the stage is being right there in the middle of it all; standing on the stage as they play around me. That's my dream.

I looked at my watch and it was coming up to half seven. I didn't know if Jonah would be on time – I doubted he would be, so I reckoned I had time to go to the loos and check on my make-up and stuff. I turned around to see Wes explaining The Venue Presents wall to Emily, who was watching him talk with a small, satisfied smile on her face. See?

Everything goes according to plan.

I walked off, past a group of chemo girls (the "next big thing", apparently – a fusion of emo and chav. Sounds useless to me. Depressed Chavs? Nuh-uh. Not good) who had just walked in, giggling and dressed in black with Nike wrist bands, baseball hats and trainers. I realized that one of them was Hannah Eveleigh, a loud-mouthed, outspoken blonde girl that I know from down my road, so I quickly ducked my head and made my way over to the girls' loos on the other side of the room, which was next to a door marked "Private".

I pushed the door open and stepped inside. The toilets are a little bit grim, but they have this amazing huge mirror over the taps that's on a bit of a slant, so you can see your entire body if you back off a bit. I reapplied my lip gloss – a girl can never have enough lip gloss – and had a good look at myself in the mirror. The girl I saw looking back at me looked nervous. She was chewing her lip and her eyes were wide. Then I realized I was a little bit nervous. But also excited. Both feelings were bubbling up inside of me, and I couldn't stay looking at myself for ever, so I took one last glance at the petite brunette with dark-lined green eyes and ripped black T-shirt, and went out into the crowd.

The place was at least half full already, some people on stage, fiddling with the amps and guitars, and some milling around and greeting each other, the air starting to buzz with expectancy – or maybe that was just me. I couldn't see Wes anywhere. The crowd was pretty thick, so I just decided to make my way over to the bar. I looked at my watch as I walked, trying to keep my feet from doing a jig to release the tension. It was just a few minutes later than we said, so I was casually late, which was good, but when I looked over to the bar I couldn't see him. My pulse picked up a fraction, but I calmed it down. He's a boy, and what is the one thing we can count on all boys being?

Late.

So I strutted with more confidence than I felt over to the bar, which I leaned on, so that I could see the door but also the

94

crowd. After all, he might have walked in, not seen me at the bar and gone to talk to a few people.

Maybe.

I was lost in my own thoughts for a bit, and then I decided to crowd-scan. I still couldn't see Wes and Emily, but the roadies had subtly come on to the stage and started to do a final tuning. That's one of the good things about The Venue: they always make sure that their acts start promptly.

I flicked my hair a bit for something to do, put on a bit more lip gloss, and then pretended to text someone, like I was a bit cool and, like, had friends, they just weren't here. Then the door opened and I jumped out of my skin and my head snapped up, but it was just a large group of kids from the year above filing in and filling up most of the extra space. The place was getting full and loud, and it made me aware that everyone was talking to someone else whilst I was stood at the bar, alone, feeling like a right gooseberry. I looked at my watch. I'd been standing there for ten minutes! It had felt like twenty. Where was he? I couldn't have missed him, surely?

"Excuse me, can I help?"

I turned around. The guy behind the bar was very cute. He had dark, messy blond hair, really toned arms and a friendly smile with a lip piercing.

Hmm, lip ring!

I pouted. "Not really."

He put down the glass he was holding and leaned forward. "Waiting for someone?"

"Hmmm," I said, not meeting his eyes.

95

Time check: ten to. The band were starting to play a bit, finishing off their tuning. Any minute they would start to play. Where was he? Was he not even coming?

I willed myself not to blurt out that I'd been stood up. I was not about to—

"Got stood up?"

Damn, was I that obvious?

"No!" I snapped, far too quickly. The blond boy laughed.

"No," I said, in calmer tones. "He's just a little bit late, is all. He'll be here soon."

"What's your name?" he asked, with a half smile that gave him a dimple in one cheek.

"Holly," I answered, surprised.

"Well, Holly, if your friend doesn't show up in the next ten minutes, how about I buy you a drink?"

Inside I was nearly crying. I must have looked really, really good or else the cute boy with a lip ring (hmm, lip ring!) wouldn't be asking me if I wanted a drink, and Jonah wasn't there to see me looking so great! I felt so stupid for making an effort for someone who couldn't even make the effort to show up.

TK, a part owner of The Venue, walked out on to the stage. The room had totally filled up now, and everyone cheered as he walked on.

"Hey, everybody! Let's get on with it. Here's the first part of the line-up for MSR! Let's hear it for The Dandys!"

The entire room erupted as the band strutted on, claimed their instruments and started their first song. The bass line and riff combined with the drums hypnotized my hips, and they wanted to dance. I looked at my watch. He was nearly twenty-five minutes late, with not so much as a text.

Screw this, I thought.

I turned to Boy-At-The-Bar.

"I'll hold you to that! I'm going to dance, see you later. . ."

"Jack." He filled the space with his name.

"Right," I smiled. "Jack! Later. . ."

Jonah obviously asked me out, and then met some other girl and just decided that I wasn't worth it. Well, he was wrong. So wrong. I pushed my way to the middle of the crowd, which is always a scary thing to do when you're a midget like me, and got near the front, listening to the set.

I don't know how long I stayed there, but I just let the crowd carry me. That's the thing with the pit – if you resist, you get hurt; but if you go with the flow and let the music carry you, the crowd is just one organism and it's all good.

I let the drums beat into my head and drum out all of the thoughts about Jonah the Pig and what he might be doing instead of being here with me. I let the bass soak into my soul and cleanse me like a steaming hot shower. I let the lead guitar take over my body and make it jump and shake and dance as hard as it could, and then I let the vocals dance around my eyes like raindrops stuck to my eyelashes. Music can be the most healing of things.

Before I knew it, the set was over and I was thirsty as hell. I headed over to the bar, and finally caught sight of Wes.

"Good set!" I exclaimed, bouncing on his shoulders as he waited to be served.

97

"There you are!" he said beaming. "I couldn't find you anywhere! I thought it would be all right, that you'd be with Jonah—"

My face must have dropped a little, because the next thing I knew he was giving me a pitying look, almost like he was expecting it. A twinge of annoyance hit my stomach, but I ignored it because I'd been alone for God-knows-how-long, and I needed to talk to him.

"Did he not show?"

I shrugged. "Nope. But it's OK, because I've got a drink waiting for me!"

And right on cue, Jack waltzed up and beamed at me.

"So, Holly – did your friend show?"

I shook my head sadly.

"One drink coming up, then, as promised!" He picked up a glass with a flourish. "What do you want?"

"J20, pink flavour?"

He winked. "Sure, anything you want."

He wandered off to the other end of the bar. Wes turned to me, blocking my view of Jack's lovely bum.

"Who's that guy?"

"Oh, that's Jack!" I replied loftily, looking down at my twisting hands. "He wanted to buy me a drink because I've been stood up." I looked up into Wes's face, which was frowning. "Oh, what, Wes?"

"You're accepting a drink off a total stranger?"

I rolled my eyes. "Sorry, big brother, I didn't realize I had to check with you first. And besides, he's not a total stranger, he's *Jack. . .*"

Wes looked like he wanted to say something, but then judging the look on my face, he just let it slide. His drinks arrived, he paid, and then turned back to me.

"So how's it going with Emily?" I asked.

He smiled, his eyes a bit distant. "Good! We danced and we've had a laugh, and now I've come to get her a drink whilst she's talking to some girls she knows."

My drink came and I smiled at Jack. "Thanks, you're an angel."

"Yeah, you could say that!" he laughed. "Are you coming next week to MSR?"

"Yep!" I nodded. "I'm going with this fine guy here!" I clapped Wes on the shoulder.

Jack nodded. "Great. If you see me there, come over and say hi. Maybe you can repay me for the drink?"

"Yeah, sure!"

Jack walked away, and Wes cleared his throat.

"Look, I've got to go, y'know, give Emily her drink, so. . ."

"OK!" I said, feeling suddenly awkward, putting a damper on my newly found good mood. Now I just felt stupid and alone again. I tried to put on a bright face. "Yeah, well, have a great night! Good luck!"

He nodded, and suddenly mingled off into the crowd. He was being all weird. Huh. Boys!

I was sipping away at my girly J20, musing dark thoughts to myself about the uselessness of boys and why we bother with them, when some big-footed, lager-ridden oaf tumbled backwards and managed to tip the entire contents of his pint glass down my brand new top. I felt the chilly liquid soak through the top layer and then into the second layer of my bra, and it splashed all into my nicely curled pretty hair.

And then to top it all off, he stood on my foot.

My mood suddenly snapped and I thought I was either going to scream or cry. I ran off in the direction of the girls' loos again, feeling utterly lost and sad. Why did Jonah not turn up? Why was Wes being distant and snappy? Why were all big tall blokes jerks?!

I burst into the girls' toilets, almost ready to cry, limping heavily and looking down my top to assess the damage, when I realized that I wasn't in the girl's bathroom.

"Have you come to get us more drinks?" asked a voice.

I paused, horrified. I knew that voice.

I looked up in disbelief.

There sat The Faeries.

No kidding.

The actual real-life Faeries, all four of them: Matt in a rocking chair, Vikki and Chevans on bean bags and the god himself, Robin Goodfellow, on his feet and staring at me with those beautiful eyes like I had just fallen out of his fridge.

And there I was: covered in beer, my hair all askew, my face reddened with embarrassment and sheer frustration and peering down my top to look at my bra.

Not how I imagined this would go.

Thoughts broke like a dam into my head. They weren't even supposed to be in Cathen yet, not until the week after! What were they even doing in The Venue? A sudden thought hit me. Oh my god – a secret gig! Amazing! I stood there frozen to the spot, feeling for the second time that night the absolute gooseberry that I am, until miraculously Vikki spoke.

"Hey, you look familiar. Do you come to a lot of our gigs?"

I couldn't speak. Wide-eyed, I nodded.

"I'm at the front of every south-west show you do," I croaked, my voice finding its way out unexpectedly. "With Wes. We're big fans."

"Oh my God, you're the kids who always wear the Superman T-shirts, right?" cried Chevans.

Oh my God. Chevans knew who I was.

"Yeah, you're the superhero chick!" agreed Matt.

Matt with the great bum.

He knew us too!

Ohmygoodness!!

"I know you now," Robin started, his devilish smile creeping on to his face. "You and your boyfriend are really cute together."

I was about to reply with a great big "Wes isn't my boyfriend, I'm single, Robin, TAKE ME!", but right then a bouncer walked in.

"Do you need any—"

Then he saw me.

"NO CIVILIANS IN THE PRIVATE ROOMS! OUT!"

And I was yanked backwards by my right arm. I just had time to wave to the band before I was escorted through the hall, down the stairs, through the entrance and out into the fresh air. It hit me like a wake-up call.

"You're banned for the night, miss," said the bouncer, stiffly. "Sorry. See you next week."

I began to walk home alone and in shock. It could only have

been half nine at the latest, so there was still a touch of pink in the sky. I realized that it was slightly chilly, and that I was still clutching my J20 tightly in my hand. Dizzily, I went over what had just happened in my head. I had been stood up, chatted up, awkward-ed out, beer-showered, celebrity-shamed and chucked out, all in the space of an hour and a half.

That was more than enough for one night, I decided, as I limped my way home.

9

I went to work on the Saturday still feeling a little bit numb from confusion. I didn't know quite how to feel – I'd obviously been stood up, but Robin "Fittest of Them All" Goodfellow had recognized me from his shows! That doesn't happen every day! But neither does a date with Jonah.

I had my iPod hidden in my pocket with one earphone in, listening to a bit of therapy. I hadn't had time to tell Wes yet, but I'd just tell him at his later. I was supposed to be going around after work, but I wasn't really in the mood to fix up someone else when I'd just been scammed. There was a hole where all my excitement and happiness had been the day before that only a large tub of half Butterscotch and malteaser, half SuperChocolate could fill.

You've shot me down
But I've realized
That I wasn't your first target.
Girls like you, you drive me wild
And it's girls like you I'd rather forget.

As I polished Ozzie's counter absentmindedly for the third time, a pair of hands appeared leaning on the counter in front of me. I looked up angrily – because this selfish person was putting greasy fingerprints on to my nice and shiny counter – ready to politely offer my services so they would get right off my lovely clean top.

Our eyes collided like a car crash.

I looked down to the top again, humiliated, and polished harder.

"Hi, how can I help?" I asked, trying to not let too much venom soak into my words.

"You could listen to my apology for why I was a jerk and didn't turn up last night?" Jonah murmured, trying to catch my eye, but I wouldn't look up into his face. I would never look at it the same way again; that evil, conniving but beautiful face. I was beginning to think that he was a bit like Angel from *Buffy*: all gorgeous and drooly on the outside, but a vampire on the inside. Vampires have a natural instinct to kill and stuff, and Jonah had a natural instinct to be a jerk. See my train of thought? Then Jonah was obviously Angel. And if he was Angel then that would make me Buffy, which I'm not going to argue about because she's a bit gorgeous, but I'd have to lay off the leather pants a bit, and do something about the nose.

But Angel and Buffy get together. Maybe we were supposed to be together, like we were destined. Like he was supposed to be a jerk and I was supposed to be a fitty, and we were supposed to be a couple.

Seeing his gorgeous, evil face had made my head turn mush again, and it made the little brain that I had so confused that it had completely abandoned my body and voice. I stopped polishing like my life depended on it, and just stood there, dumb like an empty puppet.

He slid into the high stool in front of me.

"I was going to come, I promise. I'd been looking forward to it all week! But I had to go see my granddad."

What, on a Friday? He never misses a Friday out, and so would never go to see his grandfather on a Friday! What a lame excuse! I couldn't believe that he was making up such a blatant lie and using his poor granddad as an alibi.

My anger made me snap into action.

"Yeah, of course, you were going to your granddad's!" I exclaimed with a hint of sarcasm and just a pinch of furious rage (I admired the effect, I must say) to his Greek-god face. Lip ring (hmm). Stupid bewitching lip ring! (Hmm.) You're not going to stop me! "And of course your granddad must live in some faraway land called Furthest Place Away Ever Where I Don't Have A Phone To Call My Date To At Least Be Polite So She Doesn't Look Like A Complete Wally When She Is Stood Up?" I asked.

That sentence had so much attitude that I thought I was going to morph into a cheerleader there and then, with the little attitude head-bop and clicking of fingers. I was so tempted to go, "Oh no, you did NOT!" but on second thought, maybe it was a bit much.

"It was his birthday and he'd planned for me to go around and . . ." He looked around the room, bright green eyes shining. Today they were the same green as the grass after it's rained – I'd never seen such green eyes before. When he saw that there was no one about, he leaned in conspiratorially; and before I could rebuke his slimy arm for leaning on my lovely clean counter, I leaned in myself.

Damn, the lip ring (hmm – STOP IT!) must have still been weaving its magic on me, but it was only a matter of time before I would be able to shake off its hold over me!

". . . and make toy planes with him," Jonah continued. "He used to be a pilot in the war, so loves all that stuff. I do it every year on his birthday, and this year I told him I couldn't but he forgot, and rang up my mum all upset because I hadn't arrived and he thought something had happened. He's really old and gets upset easily, so Mum made me go there instead and I forgot to take my phone. I was there all night, Holly, I'm sorry. And he does have a phone, but I didn't have your number on me, so I couldn't get hold of you."

Oh. Right. Well, it could have still been a big lie, but something about the way he was telling it – the slight frown in his brow, the cloudiness in his eyes when he spoke about his granddad going a little confused. I don't know, it all just kind of clicked into place and when he had finished talking, I believed him.

I stood there in silence, wracking my brain for something to say in response.

106

"Holly? Look, please don't be too angry," he pleaded, mistaking my dumb-blonde silence for an angry interlude. "I think we could have something special starting here. We have, y'know, like, a bond forming, sweetie, don't you think?"

I looked up into his face, which was all intense, his eyes questioning mine. I was determined not to look at the li— Ahem, the l** r***, because I was already swooning. "Something special"? "Sweetie"? Forget swooning, I was practically on the floor in a usless heap, giggling and smiling like a loon.

He shook his head, tearing his eyes from mine so quickly that it almost hurt. "Or I thought we did, before I messed up. I can't believe I've ruined this. I'm sorry I've upset you, Holly. I'd better go."

Jonah slid off his stool and made to leave. I couldn't let him go, not after a speech like that!

"Jonah, wait!"

He turned slowly, a sombre expression on his face.

"It's OK, I don't want to throw anything away!" I gushed. "I don't care that you went to see your granddad, OK? It's all right."

He smiled and turned back around to the counter. "Really?"

I nodded. "Yeah, and I'm sorry that I was harsh, I was just really embarrassed last night. It's not fun being stood up."

He came and sat back on the seat in front of me. "Well, hopefully I can make it up to you. . .?" he asked, eyes twinkling. "By going to the MSR with you? I'll buy your hot dogs and Diet Coke, and treat you like a princess?"

I laughed, elbows on the counter, leaning across towards him. "And that's how you treat a princess, is it? 'Here, yur Royal Highness, d'yeh want tomato sauce and mustard on yur hot dog or wot?'"

107

He chuckled and stroked my hair. Hmm, nice. "That's exactly right," he agreed. "That's the Tiara Treatment! So what do you think?"

"Erm, I don't know. . ." I started, but when his expression faltered, I giggled. "Of course, you loser, I'll go with you. We'll have fun."

He did his lazy half smile, eyes dancing. "Good. I guess I'll see you next week then? I still haven't found a tent yet. . ." he trailed off.

YESS!

"You will. . ." I nodded, biting my lip to stop myself from shouting, "YOU'RE GOING TO BE SHARING OUT TENT, JUST AS SOON AS I GET EMILY TO AGREE!"

"So are you coming to the gig on Friday?" I asked to give my mouth something to do.

He shook his head, eyes suddenly dark. "No, can't. I'm grounded until Saturday because I skipped maths on Monday."

Oooh, he's definitely a bad boy.

And next weekend, he's *my* bad boy.

Omigod, he might ask me to be his girlfriend! I'd be, like, the official girlfriend of a god.

Yikes!

"So I guess I'll just see you on Saturday, then?"

"I guess so."

And that's when he leaned in that little bit more and kissed me over the counter. Nothing racy, mind; just a soft kiss.

And with that he was gone from the shop, leaving me melted in a puddle on the floor.

*

"I don't believe you!"

"You've got to!" I exclaimed, laughing and taking a spoonful of ice cream. I still bought it even though things had got a million squillion times better since this morning. "I'm not kidding! They recognized us, they noticed that we always wear the superhero T-shirts and they said that we were—"

I stopped mid-sentence. I couldn't tell him that. I'd told him everything down to the exact clothes they were wearing and what they had been sitting on, but I couldn't tell him that. It was Wes! It would be weird.

"We were what?" he asked innocently.

"– we were . . . loyal." I smiled. "They thanked us for coming to all the south-west shows! I'm telling you, though, it was the best moment of my life when Robin said that I was cute!"

OK, bending the truth a little, but if he said that "we" were cute, I'm part of that "we", so technically he said that I was cute!

"I can't believe it's a week and . . ." He looked at his watch. ". . . five hours and twenty . . . four minutes until we see them."

"I know! If I fall asleep before midnight, you promise you'll wake me up?"

"You won't fall asleep, you'll be with Jonah at some rave," he mused. "So let's get this right so I understand. Now he's told you some sentimental excuse, you like him again?"

"Yeah!" I managed through a mouth of chocolate.

Wes shook his head sceptically, taking another bite of ice cream.

"I don't get women. He's been messing you around since you

fell on each other in the dark." I rolled my eyes. "And you're still going to go out with him?"

I thought for a second. He had a valid excuse for everything he messed up, so why should I be mad? He's *Jonah Jones*. I'd been dreaming about him for God knows how long. And he was gorgeous. I was lucky that he'd bothered this far, so of course I was going to go out with him!

"Well, I don't have a whole horde of boys in my wake, do I? Unless you're offering..."

Wes put his spoon down, and looked up slowly. His conker eyes were wide and Bambi-like.

"Well, I ... I..."

My face suddenly dropped. Wes didn't ... I mean, he wouldn't ... because he...

He burst out laughing. "Chill out, H, I was joking!"

I laughed too, a little nervously but also a little disappointed. Why didn't Wes want me? Humph!

"So what are we going to do about Emily?" I asked, spoon in mouth. There wasn't much ice cream left after the excitement of my Faeries news. "I mean, do we feed her to the lions? The Dynamic Duo – Mrs Stone and Sloaney – would rip her to shreds on your great oak table." There was a pause as we both imagined it. Ouch. "However! I think there's only one thing we can do, to be honest."

Wes looked hopeful. "Good, because I didn't have a clue."

"Well, I think the only thing we can do is let it happen."

Wes breathed a sigh of relief. "Oh, thank God. I don't want her to meet the Dragon – wait, did you just say 'let it happen'?

110

As in 'let the lion into the cage with that beautiful blonde that I like and see what happens'? Have you got brain freeze or are you going crazy?"

I shrugged. The real answer to that question was yes, I was going crazy (and coincidentally, I did have brain freeze) but for many different reasons.

"I thought about it today at work. We, you *and* me, bring Emily over. Your mum doesn't like me, and because she knows me hopefully I'll take the beatings for the both of us. Now doesn't that sound like a fun afternoon!"

I grimaced in an ugly fashion.

"Don't make that face, or the wind'll blow and you'll be stuck like that for ever, you uggo," he mocked. "But yes, that sounds like a real plan, Batman, kudos."

"And there's another part to my amazing plan!" I revealed, shaking my jazz hands.

Wes raised his eyebrows in question, as his mouth was full of chocolate.

"We're going to ring her and ask her to come with us to the rave and stay in our tent."

Wes nearly choked.

"What!?" he spat out. "I'm beginning to think that you *are* crazy. Don't you think it's a little bit too soon?"

"Nope," I smiled. "It's fine. Invite her with us, so it's not like it's just you and her, so she doesn't get all freaked. And we're doing this now before she gets another invite. And vis-à-vis your darling mother, The Dragon Lady: you're letting her meet Blondie because if you don't, your mother will get quite stressy at you. So you'll

111

do this, because then you'll be in her good books. And most importantly, my friend, you'll do this because it will be great to show her your amazing home, and once she has seen your jacuzzi, she'll be yours!"

I handed him the phone, grinning. "Do it."

Wes took the handset and dialled in the number from his mobile. He pressed the call button, and then turned to me in a panic.

"What am I supposed to be saying?" he whispered. "I rang too early!"

"Just tell her that you've been thinking and you thought it would be great if she came to MSR with us, and stayed in our tent!" I whispered in a rush.

"Hi, Emily?" he asked, his voice a little gruff.

Hahaha, I thought, that must be his manly voice!

As Wes continued his conversation, I only half-listened, and roamed around his room. I love Wes's room. It has a big double bed, and it's blue all over: really nice, calming blues, like you're in the sea. And there are two big squishy armchairs in his "second bedroom", which is directly linked to his "first" by a small arch. It used to be a door but Wes got rid of it because he didn't like it. In that room there's a huge flat-screen TV, his own up-to-date-with-MI5 computer and a Nintendo Wii.

Ah, Nintendo Wii. I swear that's how we burn off all the ice cream.

But the best thing about Wes's room is his photo wall. It's above his bed. So many pictures of Wes and his various friends and family from weddings, birthdays, parties, gigs – it's just a big wall of memories, with ticket stubs and all sorts as well as pictures. The best bit is the pictures of us two at the top. It starts on the left-hand side from when we became friends, and pretty much maps our friendship for the past two years. He likes photography and so takes a lot of pictures, so you could guess that the picture wall was massive! I studied it, smiling at the pictures of me and him. Robin was right – we *do* make a cute couple. . .

"Done!" he said with a flourish, and dropped the phone in front of me.

"I take it from your insane grin that she said yes?"

"She said *yes*!"

He took my hands and hauled me off his bed and stuck on his iPod. He spun me around as we danced like loons and sang our lungs out to one of our Faerie songs:

My girl
You're such a peculiar creature
You're the most permanent feature
in my so-called life.
I'd carry you around in my pocket,
If you'd just let me make you my crazy teenage wife.
These days are ours,
Let's make them last-
'Cause they're gone too soon,
fly by so fast
So my teen drama queen let's cut to the chase
Its you that I want, its you
My girl!

10

*I*turned up at school on Monday morning, ready to rock. Excitement was rising everywhere. All I could hear were kids talking about MSR, or chatting about camping, or comparing bikinis for the weekend, and I could see everyone casually mingling, finding out who was staying in whose tent. I couldn't wait until I asked Jonah! Then everyone would know! And for once I would be "Holly" instead of "The Comic Book Kid": all the boys would look at me and know me; and all the girls would be like, "Oh, Holly, you're so lucky!" and I would be like, "Yeah, I know – you're not!"

Calm, my inner cow, calm.

I went into registration, and the atmosphere was just the same. In fact, it was pretty loud in there. I saw Wes and Emily laughing in the back of the room and started walking over there. Well, it was probably more like a strut from the "everybody wants to be me" daydream.

"Miss Holly Hockers, you seem to be in a good mood today."

"Good?" I grinned as I walked up to Mr Clumfield's desk. "Not good: *epic*! It's sunny, I'm happy – what's not to be epic about?!"

He leaned back in his chair and laughed. "Oh, youth. . ." he muttered, grinning at me. "Oh, what it is like to be so easily humoured?"

"I'm humoured by that tie you're wearing!" I giggled. He was wearing a dancing banana tie, which is a tie with dancing bananas on it. Never, *ever* going to pull.

"This'll be a classic one day!" he cried, as I strutted like the super-hot chick I was (or that's what they'd be saying when they knew about me and Jonah) over to the back.

As I reached them, Emily and Wes both erupted into a fit of hysterical giggles.

"What's so funny, guys?" I asked as I sat down, vaguely registering that Emily was sat in my seat, so I was forced to sit across from them both laughing fit to burst.

When they had quite finished, Emily managed to say: "Aw, nothing, don't worry, honey, you wouldn't understand."

Ahem, excuse me? Who did she think she was?

I glanced at Wes with a quizzical look, but he just shook his head with a small smile and cast his look back to Emily. His eyes were all warm and happy, all shiny when he looked at her. My tummy grumbled and I realized that I was jealous. He only had eyes for her; he hadn't said a word to me. Humph!

"So how are you guys? Good weekend?"

"Yeah, it was pretty great!" Emily jumped in. It started to dawn on me how her voice was kind of . . . grating. A bit nasal. A bit annoying. A bit too American. "Yeah, like yesterday me and Wes went to the park, and we sunbathed and we had ice cream—"

OK, I'd heard enough. The park? In the sun? Bathing? With ice cream?

That's what we do!

That's *our* thing!

My inner cow growled. Well, if cows could growl, it would have, but I suppose it was more like a low, menacing moo. I soothed it with a few home truths. 1) She was pretty, but that was about it. There was nothing interesting about her. 2) She was interested in bad boys. Wes wasn't a bad boy. 3) She had an annoying voice.

That was about all I could muster right there and then, but they all contributed to the fact that if/when they did get together, Wes and Emily wouldn't last past the end of the summer.

So I forced a grin. "Sounds like a great Sunday afternoon!"

'Yeah, it was pretty cool." Wes smiled.

Was that the only adjective they knew or something?

"Hey, y'know what?" Wes asked me, suddenly looking up like he'd just realized I was there. "We're going over to mine after school to play a bit of Wii." He widened his eyes. "Why don't you come too? Bring someone so we can play doubles and stuff?"

I knew he meant Jonah, and I knew that this was Let's Meet

116

Mummy, and I knew that I was supposed to be happy because it meant the plan was going really well; but I couldn't help my good mood from dropping a few notches from "blinding sunshine" to "mild with a slight wind". I just couldn't shake the feeling of wanting to violently slap Emily's hand away as she batted Wes's shoulder.

So to give my hands something anti-aggressive to do, I whipped out my phone and composed a text to Jonah.

Recipient: The Fittest One
Hey. How was ur wknd?
Thnx for coming to c me
on sat, made me :) What r
u up 2 after skl? If ur free,
fancy coming to Wes' 2
play on Wii?
Send?

No, I couldn't send that – the last bit rhymed. Ahh, and was it a bit pushy to send the last bit, anyway? Stick to the "one question" rule: only ask a boy one question in a text if you want them to text back. Ask more than one and they can't be bothered to text you back, and so leave you hanging like a fool.

Re-do!

Recipient: The Fittest One
Hey. How was ur wknd?
Thnx for coming to c me

on sat, made me :) R u up
2 nythin after skl?
Send?

Oooh, now there's the kiss/no kiss dilemma!

Kiss or no-kiss?

Does a kiss seem too presumptuous or pushy, like I think we're involved? Or does it seem flirty and nice and friendly? And if I don't put a kiss, does that seem rude?

No. No-kiss seems friendly and not pushy, and also not too bothered about the whole thing! Nonchalant! It's what its all about.

MESSAGE SENT.

I spent the rest of the day split between checking my phone and sending death glares in Emily's direction. It wasn't that I wanted Wes; it was the fact that Wes was, well, mine. He was my bezzay. And the blonde bimbo was all flirty and sexy and long-leggy and all sorts, and he was spending all his time thinking about and looking at her. And Jonah hadn't texted back, so it looked like I was spending the afternoon alone.

MESSAGE RECEIVED!

(Thank god, I'd been beginning to wonder if I had even sent it!)

Time Sent: 2.59pm
SENDER: The Fittest One
Hy bbe :) Yh wknd ws gud
ta, betr 4 cin u! Sry im busy
aftr skl, gt 2 go 2 dentist :(
il b thinking of u. Cnt
wait 4 fri X

Great! I was all alone – again! I was beginning to get really angry but then reread the text and he said he'd be thinking of me, which is always nice. I couldn't wait until Friday either. It was going to be the perfect warm-up to the Best Weekend Of My Life!

So I walked out of the gates, got on to the bus, and walked down the street and then all the way up Wes's extraordinarily long drive with the two of them laughing and joking – all with my head held high. I may have been alone, but I was there to do a favour for my best friend and I was damn well going to do it! As we walked up the steps, I looked at myself quickly. Emily would definitely look good next to me! Jeans, flip-flops, bare shoulders, bare midriff, bright colours: the only way I could be more obvious is if I wrote "Bully me, Mrs Stone, please!" across my chest. I pinned a smile on to my face. It was going to be fine. It wasn't as if she was nasty exactly, it was just that she ignored my very presence! Hmm.

"This is my house!" Wes said with a flourish as he pushed open the heavy door.

"Woah!" Emily exclaimed. "Nice place. I have a staircase like

119

that! Or I did in my house in the US. OMG, is that, like, a crystal chandelier?"

I was nodding and smiling along on the outside, but inside I was pacing around. Where was Mrs Stone? She usually appeared straight on the dot when the door opened, to see who was entering. But I couldn't see her stunning yet devilish form, I couldn't hear her lethal heels, I couldn't smell her Chanel – where was she? It was making me nervous.

We moved around into the great white kitchen, which was chrome and tiles as far as the eye could see; the library, looking like something out of *Beauty and the Beast*; the study, lounge, second lounge, bathroom, washroom, cloakroom, games room, conservatory – and she wasn't in any of them. We headed upstairs.

"And this is Juanita's quarter," Wes was saying, as we followed like sheep in his wake along the landing. "She's our maid. She's Spanish and doesn't speak loads of English, but she's funny and a really good cook!" We heard a rattling in her kitchen, the sound of something being dropped into the metal sink. "That might be her now, actually!"

We trooped into the small kitchen, me first. Juanita wasn't there. Instead, in the corner, stood Mrs Stone.

"Mother." Wes's tone suddenly stiffened. "What're you doing in here?"

Mrs Stone smiled, but it wasn't her usual superior, smug smile; it was too tight and forced. She never came into that kitchen: she made a point of it.

"Simply checking that Juanita is keeping her quarters spick

and span, dearest," she declared, not missing a beat. Her eyes flicked over me quickly in distaste, and then straight on to Emily. She smiled juicily. "However, dear, the question here is, who is this darling girl and why have you not brought her home before?"

Emily smiled demurely, which was extremely out of character for her normally extroverted approach. "Well, how do you do, Mrs Stone? I hope I find you well this afternoon."

I was so surprised; she was acting less like her usual "How're ya doing?" Wink-And-A-Smile Barbie, and more like Shy, Respectable And PC Barbie. I actually thought for a fleeting moment that she was going to bob down into a curtsey, but before she did, Mrs Stone walked over and did something I'd never seen her do before, to either of her children: she placed a perfectly manicured claw (oops, I mean hand!) on to Emily's shoulder. Even Wes looked surprised.

"My dear girl," she cooed. "I am most well, as I trust you are. You are simply beautiful, darling; you must be Emily, whom my Margo was talking of! She was right, your hair is stunning; what a delightful shade of blonde!"

I backed away a bit, stunned. So the plan went a little better than expected – but I didn't know that The Dragon was capable of saying nice things. I leaned back against the counter for support, and my metal belt clicked loudly on something. It made me turn around to have a look, and I saw that it was only the metal sink. I was about to turn around, but then I saw what was in the sink. A spoon. But not just a spoon – a spoon with a chocolate-looking slush melting on it that looked suspiciously like—

That's why she was in here, looking uneasy and pouring out the compliments! She'd been at the ice cream!

I looked back to Mrs Stone, my eyes wide. My head was spinning. I'd thought the ice cream had been going down, bit by bit, but Wes and I had just assumed that Juanita had been having a bit every so often. But Mrs Stone didn't like food, let alone ice cream. I'd never seen her eat. And she always said that she didn't like ice cream; she made out like she was some kind of martyr for it, she didn't even have it in the house—

Because she would eat it all!

I'd found out Mrs Stone's guilty secret.

I gasped.

They all looked at me.

"You all right, Hols?" Wes asked, concerned.

I couldn't help myself. I looked over to Mrs Stone, and her dark, lifeless eyes suddenly awoke at the sight of my own wide, shocked ones. They took in the sink, my expression, and put two and two together. It was then that I saw the first flicker of humanity I would ever see in Wes's mother: panic.

I cleared my throat.

"Um-hum, yeah, I'm good. I just, er, forgot to breathe!"

What was I on about?! I needed to get away from that mind-numbing stare.

"So how about that Nintendo Wii, ey?" I suggested to a wide-eyed Wes. "Can't wait to play that tennis!"

I was using all of my subliminal power to get Wes out of the room so I could tell him about his façade of a mother, but he wasn't getting the urgency. Boys never get the urgency.

"Yeah, it's pretty cool!" Wes said to Emily, smiling, unaware of the tension building between his mother and myself. "It's in my room. . ."

We all turned to leave. Wes left first, then Emily, then me – but just as I thought I was free, a claw snapped out and grasped my arm like a vice. Emily and Wes continued down the corridor, chatting away about something cheery, like they were in their own little world, and I turned to face the devil herself. Up close, Mrs Stone wasn't that pretty. The skin around her eyes looked tired and despite the surgery, wrinkles were catching up with her. And those eyes looked huge and threatening, the pupil and iris all one colour, and I felt like they were going to swallow me up whole.

"Tell anyone, and you never come around to this house again. Do you hear me, girl?" she hissed into my ear with words that flew. "And if you do, you can say goodbye to your tent for the silly festival this weekend, because you won't even be going. I paid for your tickets; I can get them cancelled."

I was that shocked that my knees almost gave way. It was too much information to take in in only a few moments. Before I knew it, Mrs Stone had escorted me down the hall, hands on my shoulders – her talons digging in like a great bird of prey – to Wes's room.

"You don't look too well, dear. Maybe you should go home? Tell Winston you're leaving. And while you're leaving things, do leave him alone. He has finally found a young lady who is worthy of his time and efforts – someone at the same level, someone *good enough* for him. I hope you understand."

123

Then, without another word, Mrs Stone straightened up and walked off down the corridor, leaving me stunned into silence and stuck to the ground, wondering what the hell I should do.

11

So I just walked in and told Wes I was sick, and that I had to go home. It didn't even look like he was that bothered. All I could see was him looking at her in all her perfection: her beauty, her humour, her wealth.

And then I really did feel sick.

I went home and I cried like I had never cried before. Y'know when you cry, but you're not really sure what you're crying for? It felt like that. I'd never thought that I wasn't good enough to be someone's friend before; it had never crossed my mind. Her voice when she said that phrase: "someone *good enough*" – it was like I'd been wrapped in this nice big cloak that was keeping me so warm from the snow, but then suddenly that cloak got stripped away, and I was stood shivering in the freeze, blinking back the icicles and wondering how on earth I was going to live without it.

Mum brought up a cup of tea and tried to get me to tell her what was wrong. She even woke up Dad. But I couldn't put it into words: my mind wouldn't work. I would try to talk, and then I would just hear Emily's laugh in my head, or see her face, and jealousy would explode so violently in the pit of my stomach that the words were blown clean away, leaving only a thick coating of self-loathing. I couldn't even listen to our favourite song. I stuck on a different CD so I didn't have to listen to my own thoughts.

I know, that
You know
You've got a hold around
Me that
Nobody else could
Know.
Your idle heart
For my
Idle soul, the
Ideal trade,
I've been
Told.

The rest of the week was spent with me not saying much, and not doing much. Tuesday I had a bad headache from all the crying and when people talked to me I flinched, so when they

126

asked me what was wrong I just said I had a migraine. All that day I watched Wes and Emily. They were friendly with each other, laughing and joking – and it occurred to me that I had never actually seen them talking, like *really* talking, like we do. But then I suppose he chooses his friends to talk with and his girls to—

Whatever.

But I just couldn't help thinking that I must be pretty awful to not be as good as her, someone who can't even hold a conversation. But we hadn't actually had a real conversation for a while, what with all the Emily/Jonah stuff going on – we each had someone to focus on apart from each other.

Stuff with Jonah was going well. He texted me on the Tuesday, but I didn't reply, and when I bumped into him at school on Wednesday I told him I had the mother of all headaches, and he gave me a hug in front of everyone (Jonah doesn't really "do" hugs, whereas I'm a pretty huggy person – I'd hug a fish if it wouldn't, like, die, as soon as you took it out of the water) but I couldn't even get excited about it. The week had lost its rosy glow and I felt a bit out of it.

"Darling, do tell me why you've got a face like a slapped arse – it's *so* last season."

Margo wasn't helping either. She kept on finding little opportunities to talk to me during the week to try to find out why I had lost my mojo, and why I was "a bit out of sorts" with Wes.

He'd been trying to talk to me all week. Well, I say "talk" – all he wanted to do was ask me about Emily. Had she said anything?

Was she excited about the weekend? Did I know if she liked Cubical or Hyperbowl better? He asked me round to dinner and a movie-fest on the Wednesday night. The thought of seeing his mum made me want to be ill in the nearest bin, and besides, I couldn't take another few hours of "Emily *this*, Emily *that*" – I'd sooner eat the next-door-neighbour's kamikaze cat than put myself through it. I couldn't summon up the energy to be helpful any more, and I snapped at him on that Wednesday afternoon – saying that I didn't know if she preferred to be kissed with eyes open or not because I'd helped him to get to the point where things could start to happen, and now he had to do just that: make it happen.

"I'm not your relationship guru, Wes! Just grow a pair and *get on with it!*"

I may have been a little bit harsh, but it meant he stopped twittering on about how amazing Emily was.

By Thursday night I was beginning to lose sight of the happiness. I was deliberating whether to drop into the hole where everything is dark and gloomy, with a heavy metal-scremo soundtrack and wearing a lot of black (i.e., to have an "emo day"), when my mum came into my Hall of Pain and Mental Angst (my room) and held out the phone.

"It's for you," she whispered, smiling mysteriously, and then left the room and shut the door.

"Hello?"

"My beautiful Holly, I haven't seen you since Saturday! Nearly a whole week! Are you all right?"

It was Ozzie.

Bless him.

I took a deep breath.

"Thanks, Ozzie, I'm fine! I'm sorry – this week's been so busy I haven't had much time. . ."

Busy wallowing and not going anywhere or doing anything. I was beginning to get a bit bored, to be honest.

"Well, I wonder if you would be free this evening? I would need a hand?"

Hmm. He was concerned for me. He needed some help at the shop. He'd always been there for me, so I should be there for him. Also, I hadn't eaten ice cream since Monday because the thought had made my headache return, but I had started to get withdrawal symptoms and I just knew that Ozzie's comforting conversation and iced dairy treats would at least make me feel a teensy bit better.

"Of course," I said softly, with a smile. "I'll come and help. I'll be down in ten minutes."

I was down in five. Suddenly my appetite had come back, and I needed to wallow with people rather than by myself before I developed multiple personalities. (The plus side to that was that if I did create a few, maybe one of them would be good enough to be around Wes.)

I opened the door, and there – sat comfortably at the bar – was Wes. He was chatting to Ozzie across the counter, and when Ozzie waved me over from the door and he turned to see who it was, he looked equally surprised, smiled, but didn't do his usual wave. He didn't know how to act around me. I suddenly felt a pang of guilt. Who cared if his monster mother didn't think that I was good enough? He didn't even like her! He chose me to be his friend, and why should it matter if she didn't approve? And as for Emily — hmm. I still didn't like her. Well, I wasn't going to think about Emily just yet.

I made my way over to the bar and sat down next to Wes.

"What are you doing here?" I asked, smiling.

"I was about to ask you the same thing!" Wes declared, and smiled wider, as I wasn't scowling or shouting or being, y'know, my nasty self.

"I'm supposed to be covering a shift for Ozzie." I turned to Ozzie and smiled.

Wes paused suspiciously. "Me too."

We both looked at Ozzie for an explanation, and to our surprise he burst out laughing.

"Kids!" he cried, laughing. "Ah-ha, crazy kids, Ozzie fools you!"

When he had calmed down, he made things clear.

"I want to surprise you, see?"

We looked at each other, confused. We did not see.

"You know that the Midsummer Rave you are going to this weekend, for it you must have, to get right close to the bands, a ticket?"

"What?!" Wes and I shouted at the same time.

"I didn't know that!" I turned to Wes. "Oh my God, I don't believe it! Did you know?"

Wes shook his head. "No, I didn't, I just presumed you showed up and saw everything. Damn!"

I was so angry that I hadn't checked if you needed a pass for the pit. Now we wouldn't get to the bar and we wouldn't be able to be right up close, all in the action; we'd have to sit with all the lame people who didn't want to dance or, y'know, have *fun*.

We sat in a shocked silence for a few seconds, as Ozzie pulled out an envelope from under the counter. We both looked up at his happy, chuckling face.

"I did not think that you were, how you say, '*in the know*', so I thought Uncle Ozzie would help. . ."

He said it with a shrug, pulling two tickets out of the envelope. He handed us one each.

"For you, the superheroes, yes?"

We both squealed like girls and jumped on Ozzie, saying thank you about a million times until we both went hoarse with the happiness.

The happiness spilled into Friday. My mojo was back and working, so I could even manage to smile to Emily and hold back the instinct to bite and scratch her (funnily enough, very much like the kamikaze cat next door) which I thought was a bonus. And Jonah had texted me early Friday morning:

MESSAGE RECEIVED!

Time Sent: 7.17am
SENDER: The Fittest One
Mornin hockerz — 2nites the
nite! Call u l8r, hv a gr8
dy:) XX

I was really happy about it, but the thing was . . . I had this feeling. A nag at the back of my mind. Jonah was gorgeous, no doubt, and I'd wanted him for ages. But now he was there, it was kind of . . . all right. He was texting me, I wasn't texting him. He was chasing me a bit, not the other way around. I didn't know! It was just kind of weird. I thought it would be great to have someone texting me – and he had been texting me all week – but it wasn't all that amazing. And his texts weren't all that interesting: "Wt r u up 2?" or "Im bord, wt u up 2?" or "Maths sux. Thinkin of u. Wt r u up 2?" But still, Jonah Jones, gorgeous, godly boy – texting me? It could only be epic times!

School ended with a huge buzz. All the kids flew out in a dizzy mess about the music over the weekend, and who was going with who, and who would get with who, and what would generally happen. The buzz was infectious and lifted my mood that extra notch, which helped me to tolerate Wes on the phone on the way home; I assured him for the third time that I would be wearing my superhero top to the gig too, so that he wouldn't look stupid on his own. I got in and decided to have a bath and have a bit of a girly beauty sesh, so I cranked up the volume and locked myself in the bathroom for about two and a half hours of me-time. I came out at about quarter past six, ready to get ready, strutting into my room and singing along to my iPod.

I suppose you're just a bit fit, really. . .
My mum would say that you're, lovely. . .
That makes me just a bit, lucky. . .

'Cause I'm the one who takes you out,
'Cause I'm the boy you care about
'Cause I'm the guy who's your cup of tea
And you're the only girl who's right for me!

Well, it's less of a singing-song, and more of a shouty, jumpy-up-and-downy, wake-up-your-baby-sister-if-she's-sleeping song, if I'm honest.

"Holly, will you shut off that racket!" Mum cried as she rushed into my room, all dressed up except for her make-up. "You'll wake up Lizzy!"

Just as she barged in, the phone rang. I turned down my music so it was just a low blip of guitar and drums, and picked it up. I'd put it next to my bed just in case Jonah rang the home phone, so he wouldn't have to talk to my crazy sister if she managed to pick up the phone somehow (happens more often than you would think) or worse, my crazy mum. I took a deep breath.

"Hello?" I asked, dropping my voice so it sounded a bit sexy. Ish.

"Hi, it's Emma Bradbury, the babysitter?" she declared in peachy tones that were laced with confusion. "Who's that?"

"Oh, erm, hi Emma!" I said, my voice at my normal register. "Sorry, its Holly! I was just, er, coughing! Anyway, here's Mum!"

I passed on the phone to her.

"Oh, hi Emma! How are you? . . . Good, good, so what time will you. . . Oh – right."

I looked up at her tone. It wasn't good. Mum frowned.

"Well, I suppose broken arms heal! All gymnasts have accidents! . . . Well, get better soon!"

She put down the phone, and I knew what she was going to ask me before she even opened her mouth. Dad had the weekend off (Friday to Sunday) so they had decided to go out into the city to see a show, and then have a lazy start to the morning and a quiet weekend with me gone. It had been planned for ages because Dad doesn't get much time off, and I knew they had been really looking forward to it.

Mum gave me That Look. The look parents give you when they want you to do something for them. She opened her mouth but I cut her off desperately.

"Can't you ask anyone else?" I pleaded. "Is there no one else who will babysit?!"

Mum shook her head. "Next door won't take her from when she tried to strangle their cat, and Rosie Roberts is away in Cornwall." She pouted. "Please, Hols? I'll pay you. You said that you needed a bit of extra cash!"

"Mum, you know I've had this planned for *ages*. It's been booked for *months*!"

"So had this!" she cried, sitting on the edge of my bed.

"But The Faeries are playing! *Everyone* is going to be there!"

"I thought these fairy people were playing tomorrow, and that everyone is going to be there then? Hols, this is the only time I get to see your father. I don't get to see him much as it is! We never go out! We never get to do anything fun! We never have anywhere to go to, except PTA meetings or to the pub quiz every once in a blue moon. . ."

She'd gone off into a little world of her own, thinking about stuff. The look on her face was pitiful. I thought she was going to cry.

I took a deep breath.

"Twenty quid," I muttered.

"*What?*" she exclaimed. "You've got to be—"

"Twenty quid," I stated solemnly. "Or no deal."

Mum sat there for a second, then answered.

"Fine, twenty quid, you extortionate little minx. I'll leave it on the counter. . . Thank you."

She kissed my forehead and ran out of the room to get on her make-up like an excited school girl, and I set about texting people.

Recipient: The Fittest One
Mum jst said that I've
got to babysit, no way
I can get out of it. Argh! I'm
so sorry! Wel just have 2 have
our dance tmz :P Oh yeh, do
u want to stay in our tent? :)
Sorry again! X
Send?

MESSAGE SENT.

Recipient: The Best Friend
Mum jst said that I've
got to look after demon sis,

135

no way I can get out of it!
Argh! I'm so annoyed! >:|
Send?

MESSAGE SENT.

A few minutes later:

MESSAGE RECEIVED!

Time Sent: 6.29pm
SENDER: The Fittest One
Bbe tht sux!): Bt we cn
dance 2mz, nw. Yh share
tent! Ta gorjuss. C u then XX

But nothing back from Wes. Mum and Dad left, both gushing with thanks. I dried my hair and put on my pyjamas sadly, trying not to think about all the fun that everyone would be having, and all the music, and Matt with his guitar, and Vikki with her bass, and—

The doorbell.

I opened the door and there stood Wes. Smiling. With ice cream.

I thought I was going to cry!

"Wes!" I exclaimed, hugging him. "Oh my God, that's so sweet, I can't believe you're blowing off the gig to keep me company! You're just the *best*—"

136

Wes prised me away gently.

"Actually," he said, "I've just come to give you this." He gestured to the ice cream and then awkwardly rubbed the back of his neck. "Emily's waiting round the corner for me. . ."

I took the ice cream, punched him in the arm and shut the door in his face.

Men, huh?

Who'd have 'em!

12

I woke up after having an awesome dream, where the sun was shining and the music was raving and everyone was having a really awesome time, so I jumped out of bed, threw open my curtains and saw—

Rain?

I couldn't believe it! I'd been so focused on everything else that I just presumed our gorgeous weather would be continuing, but no! Rain! OK, so it wasn't full on chucking-it-down rain, but it was still a drizzle, and even though I could see the bright blue sky underneath the cloud, my spirits were dampened. Of course, they had already been dampened by the fact that The Faeries had played last night at The Venue and I had missed it. I sighed as I heaved myself out of bed. I bet they'd had an awesome time, and I'd missed it all.

I'd packed my bag at the end of my non-eventful evening (after the *Friends* reruns were finished) and Wes was bringing the tent, so I didn't really have anything to worry about. I jogged out of my room and hit the showers, wishing that the rain would stop by the time I'd got out. When I got into the bathroom I couldn't stop myself from breaking into a huge grin: it was Saturday, the Saturday I had been waiting for for weeks – I was going to see The Faeries at midnight tonight! And it was nine a.m. – I would be watching my most favourite band in the world perform live in less than twenty-four hours! The thought made me light up inside, though I still wished I'd been there last night. Wes had rung me during some of our songs, but all I could really hear was the band in the background and Wes's voice going hoarse as he sang along with the rest of the heaving crowd. I wanted more than anything to be there and all I could think about was how they would be having a fantastic time without me and I bet they didn't even miss me, but the thought that had kept me going was MSR and how amazing it was going to be, and now the day was here! The day we'd been talking about for months, the huge gig that we had been preparing for – all those hours learning the new album, and listening to the old album, and repairing our T-shirts. . .

When I got out of the shower, I pulled my H'y Girl T-shirt out of the wardrobe. It's my favourite item of clothing by far – Wes and I made them ages ago just before our first Faeries gig, and we've tried to wear them to every gig since. They were blue, like the Superman T-shirts, but instead of the big "S" in the middle, mine had "H'y Girl" and his had "Lameboy" squished into the triangle. They're pretty cool! And then on the back is all of the gigs we've

139

been to: date, place and tour. It smelt like summer – freshly cut grass and sunshine. I'm not quite sure how it could smell like sunshine, but it just did! I put it on with some white shorts and instantly felt good, and when I looked outside, the sky had started to clear up! Result!

The bands were starting at midday and gates opened at ten, and considering the site is only ten minutes away, Wes said he'd come and get me at about quarter past ten so that we could put up the tent. Jonah was getting a lift with some kids he knew who were setting up and working at the rave for the weekend, and I had no idea how Emily was getting there. She'd probably sprout wings and fly, the perfect little—

"Are you off, Berry?" a croaky voice asked from my parents' bedroom.

They'd got in late last night, but it had been worth it because they were both so happy and giggling like kids that they had forgotten that they had already paid me, so paid me again! I took one ten just in case I desperately needed it, and left the other ten on the counter. I'd tell them later. Just . . . not right then.

I knocked first and then pushed their door open slowly. They both looked shattered. I smiled.

"Yes," I whispered. "My phone's charged, I've got a spare pair of pants, and I've got my rape alarm, blah blah blah. I'll be fine, so don't worry about me. Have a great weekend, guys, I'll see you tomorrow!"

"Have a great time, beautiful girl," Dad smiled. Mum grumbled something.

"What was that?" I whispered.

"Your mother says that she loves you, to be careful, and that she hopes you and Wes have a great time. Speaking of Wes, I haven't seen much of him lately. Are you two OK?"

"Yeah, he's fine," I said, slightly annoyed. "But why does everyone say that, 'Are you two OK?', like we're a couple? Y'know, we don't go around joined at the hip! He's gone off and got his girl now, so we're just not all that chummy. So what? I can do stuff without him," I stammered thinking about last night and how I was really alone. "I don't need him." I thought about how he brought me ice cream and how happy I had been to see him. "I'm just fine without him . . ." I trailed off. I wasn't fine without him I missed him being close and at my beck and call.

Damn.

"Holly?"

I snapped out of my thoughts.

"Yeah, Dad?"

"Shut up and go. We love you. Call us when you want picking up."

I shut the door, smiling, just in time for the doorbell to ring! I grabbed my bag and ran out the door, and straight into Wes's chauffeured car.

"Morning, sailor!" I cried as I jumped into the back. "How are we – oh, erm, feeling?"

I turned around to see that I had just plonked myself down next to Margo. Who was dressed to kill. Big shades, cute black spangly top, chinos, designer sandals – this girl had it all. I'd forgotten the minor detail that Wes was her twin so they would more than likely be coming in the same car. Damn.

She didn't smile, but I didn't expect her to.

"Hello Margo, Finn."

"Yah, safe, mate."

Ooh, a new word!

"Good morning, Holly dearest. Such a shame you didn't make it last night, it was quite the set. We all had a fab time – mostly Jonah, I daresay! He had to prise the girls off himself, it was quite the spectacle—"

"How are you, Hols?" Wes said loudly and pointedly from the front seat with a huge grin on his face. He was also wearing his superhero T-shirt.

I grinned back. I couldn't help myself! The overwhelming sense of joy even overtook the urge to biff Margo over the head with my sleeping bag and break her stupid designer glasses in half!

"I'm great, ta, babe. Ready to get that tent up and start raving!"

When we pulled up outside the field, you couldn't see much because it was obscured by bush, fence and a ticket port-a-cabin. Margo suddenly lowered her glasses.

"And this is *it*, is it?" she asked, her voice wavering slightly.

"Yarh, darrhling!" I mimicked as I stepped out of the car and swung my back pack on to my back. "Welcome to your room! It's not quite five star, but you get what you pay for!"

Margo and Finn decided that they would share a different tent to us, which was fair enough. I was sharing a compartment with Emily (oh, what fun times! Not) and Wes was sharing with Jonah. Not the best matched in the world, but it meant I was close to Jonah and Wes was close to Emily. However, I was looking forward to seeing Margo try to put up her tent, and took great delight in her stepping out of the car and straightening herself up, and then looking around with distaste.

There was a queue to get into the site; the whole thing was barred off with makeshift metal fences, and to get in you had to go through the gates. Excitement bubbled all around me in the many faces I didn't know – some kids who had obviously come for the heavier tunes (all dressed in black with big fringes); the kids who had come for the Disco Shed (rave tunes all night in the biggest shed you've ever seen – the rave kids come in neon, so you always know which are which); and all the folk in between. I saw a few faces I knew from previous shows, and a few acquaintances that I waved to, but I couldn't stop to talk because I was too anxious to get inside. However, we did see the Mortimer brothers at the front of the queue with the Lady-Killer Squad; Matt saw us and hit James, who hit Chris, who was inhaling a hot dog. When they had all seen us, they waved and shouted madly for us to come and join them, but we had to pass and head on to the back because the glares from the die-hard fans were a bit too much.

But the queue didn't take long. It moved pretty fast, and before we could even get through an entire song on my iPod we were at the front of the queue getting our tickets checked and being given wristbands. Wes and I got purple ones, because we had the pit passes – bless Ozzie, the best honorary uncle in the world! We put them on and then were ushered inside the gates, and the whole scene suddenly came into view.

The huge stall in the next field; the hundreds of tents in the field on the other side, making the whole place look like a multicoloured, huge, bumpy carpet that spread on for ever. The huge food trucks, emitting crazy smells – Chinese, Indian, pizza, burgers, hot dogs . . . I began to drool. I could taste the hot dogs then and there, along with freshly mown grass and the smell of hundreds of people in the same confined space, an attractive taste that stung my tongue, that frightened yet elated me. The Disco Shed (literally a shed in which there are mini disco raves) and a whole mess of other stalls and makeshift bars were set up in the field we walked into. Massive speakers loomed over every end of the huge space, blaring out radio tunes non-stop. It was so loud that the ground vibrated beneath my feet! It was phenomenal. The air sizzled, practically alive, but it wasn't just that – it was also the sheer amount of people that were there already, hordes and hordes of people, all talking and screaming and singing and shouting. A riot of colour and noise, smells and tastes; my head was spinning and excitement was oozing through every fibre of my being.

"The bloke at the door just said that they had to open at quarter to because there were so many people here early that they were blocking the road!" Wes exclaimed. "Crazy, right!"

It was crazy. The whole atmosphere was crazy. It was like nothing I had ever experienced before. The buzz was so intoxicating that it didn't even feel like I was still in this world, let alone England, let alone Cathen! It was like Christmas joined with all of my birthdays, joined with prom and with every gig I'd ever been to. Nothing seemed to matter any more. I felt light, weightless. It was wild!

"This is so weird," I explained to Wes as we just stood for a moment and watched the world go by. "This atmosphere, it just makes me feel like . . ." I looked at Wes. He had a stray curl on his forehead. It looked so soft that I had the sudden urge to play with it. I reached out, feeling dreamy. ". . . anything could happen, y'know. . .?"

"Hockers!"

Jonah appeared at my side and scooped me into a tight hug. I almost couldn't breathe. I looked over his shoulder at Wes, who cleared his throat and looked away, uncomfortable.

"Jonah, hi!" I managed through my breaking ribcage. "How's it going?"

"Great! All right, Wes, mate?" he said, smiling lazily. Wes grunted in reply. I didn't know if I was just feeling strange from the sudden heat that had appeared after the rain, or if I was imagining things, but Jonah didn't look as gorgeous as I remembered. His green eyes weren't as sparkly, his hair looked over-styled, and his smile looked like he had been practising it in the mirror for hours so that it looked "cool", which somehow made it really, really uncool.

"Y'want me to carry your bag?" he offered, not waiting for a reply but just picking it up. "I bagsed us a place right over here, a real good spot. . ."

He wandered off, expecting Wes and me to follow him, so we did. I caught him up, just as he was saying:

". . .so when she said that she couldn't get a lift, I said that she could come in the car with me and Adam—"

"Who's this?" I asked brightly.

Jonah pointed to a spot about twenty metres away. "Oh, sorry, did you not hear? Emily."

She waved coyly, stood next to her large pink duffle. It was pretty big, considering it was just for the night. I briefly wondered if it had a hairdryer in it. Before I knew it, I was being attacked by a mane of long, blonde hair: Emily was hugging me! What was she playing at? She never hugged me!

"Hey, Hols, so nice to see you! Gosh, I always forget how short you are! Sorry you couldn't come last night, bummer, right?"

She didn't look bummed at all, the lying fake-baked giant. Everyone knows that short girls are prettier, anyway.

I forced myself to nod. "Yeah, bummer! Good job I'm here now, though. Let's do the tent!"

Wes grinned, rubbing his hands together. He'd been eager to do it for real, since we'd put it up in his back garden ages ago. "Yeah, let's do it!"

Emily's face fell a little as hard work loomed. "Well, I've just got to go to the bathroom! But I'll be back ASAP, right?"

She bounced off, but then flicked her long, shiny, shampoo-advert hair back to face us.

"Err, where am I going?" she giggled.

Jonah dropped my bag heavily at my feet.

"Women!" he declared to Wes. "Its all right, I'll show her. We'll be back in a bit!"

And he ran off, leaving Wes and me with a few tent poles and a big sheet. Margo stalked past with Finn in tow, carrying her bag, the tent, his bag and a large bottle of Evian. God, she's so not festival material.

"Been left already? Well, dears, maybe you're better without them!"

She waved royally as she carried on walking past, turning heads as she went, off to find a space to put their tent. No doubt they would have a small picket fence to go around the outside, equipped with some kind of device that kept people away. She really continues to surprise me, that girl.

So we started putting up the tent. Everyone around us was doing the same thing. I saw one boy hitting another with a pole; a girl sitting in tears in a crumpled mess of tent poles whilst her friend was chatting up one of the boys in the next tent to help them set up; and a bunch of people laughing and joking as they gave up with their tent and just danced on top of it to the song coming out of the speakers.

I picked up the instruction leaflet. It was in German. Hmm. I chucked it over my shoulder and picked up a pole instead and pointed it at Wes in a fencing stance.

"Mr Stone —" I cried, "— are you ready?"

To the sound of various rave/chav/punk songs from all over the field, we managed to put up the tent. It didn't take as long to do as we originally thought — it turns out those Germans make stuff pretty simple nowadays! It was actually really fun, us working together in the sun, messing around and having a laugh. We hadn't done that in ages. We got lost under the sheet, and Wes managed to crack me on the head with a pole; we did some 20s-style dancing with some poles to some heavy-metal punk — it was funny! But finally, after I had got the main pole the wrong way around and managed to almost wreck everything, Wes fixed it and we ended up with a rather cool-looking tent. It was only when we stood back to admire our (oh, all right, Wes's) handiwork that we realized Emily and Jonah weren't back.

"I bet they've got lost!" I smiled easily. Wes nodded, but also frowned. "What's wrong?"

He snapped out of it. "Nothing, H'y Girl! D'you want to go find them?"

We set off across the field to the port-a-loos, but they weren't anywhere and it was getting close to midday, so I texted Jonah to tell him that we were going to see the first band and that they should come and meet us at the back of the field. We made our way with the crowd of people into the large field where the stage was. At the sight of it I couldn't wait for midnight to arrive. A whole twelve hours away! I didn't know if I could wait that long; the excitement was driving me crazy!

We found a spot next to a very visible tree, and in a few moments Emily and Jonah arrived, laden with food. Jonah sat down next to me and handed me my hot dog.

"One luxurious meal fit for a princess, as promised!" he grinned, and tucked into his own.

"Thanks!"

Emily gave a hot dog to Wes, and looked at me. "I'm sorry we didn't get you any onions," she said with an apologetic smile. "They looked really greasy, and I didn't know if you were watching your weight. . ."

She trailed off and looked at my legs. I almost dropped my hot dog. I couldn't believe she'd just said that; my legs were absolutely fine! I looked at both of the boys to see if they'd reacted in any way, but both were engrossed (gross being the operative word) in their hot dogs. So I just forced a sweet smile.

"No, I'm not, but I don't like onions anyway – they make me feel *violently sick*," I managed through gritted teeth, trying not to glare at her. This girl was either incredibly stupid, or just trying to rub me up the wrong way. From the glint in her ever-blue eyes, I suspected the latter. I was not liking this girl, not at all – not one bit.

After we had finished our hot dogs, the bands started to play about an hour later than planned. We all just sat there and enjoyed the music and the sun, chatting to the people sat next to us, and anyone from school who came over to see us.

"Lay-deez," Matt supplied, as he sat down with the Lady-Killer Squad. They sat with us for a while, all the time staring at Emily's legs like they had just fallen from the sky, and only left when we told them someone was giving out free beer to underage kids on the other side of the field. Seriously, those boys had been kicked in the head with one too many footballs in their time.

During the third set, Jonah saw a friend and went over to say hi, and must have got lost in the crowd because he didn't come back, but I wasn't that bothered. I had just spent the afternoon with my head resting on his lap, with him stroking my hair, or us just having a chat, which didn't amount to much. I asked him about school, and he didn't say much, except: "It's rubbish, I hate it." I asked him about his house: "It's rubbish, I hate it." Family? "They're all right." Like I said, not the most thrilling of

149

conversations, so when he vanished I thought it was the perfect opportunity to take a look around.

"Wanna go dance for a bit?" I asked Emily and Wes.

Emily had lain down to sunbathe. She had her magnificently long legs out and her flat stomach bronzing in the midday sun, and every boy who walked past walked that little bit slower, just to get an extra look.

"Yeah, sounds good!" Wes exclaimed. "Coming, Em?"

She shook her head. "No, I'm sunbasking."

I smirked. "Don't you mean 'sunbathing'?"

She opened her eyes. "Nah, girls 'sunbask'; only men sunbathe, Hockers."

That nickname didn't sound as nice from her lips as it did from Jonah's. She made it sound derogatory. Bitchy. Mean.

I looked to Wes, but he still wasn't getting any of this; the stupid, subtle bullying that was going on. Blind and oblivious, that's our Wes!

We went off into the throng where the music was loud and the air was hot, and I started to move. We jumped up and down to the last few songs of an amazing punk-rockish set by a new-to-the-scene band, The LEDs, and applauded like crazy. I grinned wildly at Wes — his hair was all crazy and face shiny with a mental grin plastered to his face, but I didn't suppose I looked any better. I knew what he was thinking — this was worth the wait. And twenty minutes later, when a Latin-rave fusion band came on, we hauled ourselves up again and started to dance. I started a bit of hip rolling and Latino dancing, and then looked at Wes and almost died laughing. He had his concentration face on (i.e., scrunched-up eyes and tongue sticking out), arms up in the air, and he looked like he was playing with a hula hoop. Apart from the fact that he didn't have the hoop, Wes isn't the biggest dancer, it's got to be said. But by the time I had stopped laughing and he was just starting to the hang of it, he felt his phone ring.

Wes looked up at me, shocked.

"It's nearly six o'clock!" he yelled in my ear. We'd been away for hours! "We should probably get back!"

I nodded, and we made our way back across to where we had been sitting before. Emily and Jonah were sat with their heads close together, talking about something. As we approached, they pulled away and waved.

"Where'd you get off to?" Jonah asked, pulling me on to his lap. "I came back and you were gone!"

"Oh, we just went for a bit of a dance!" I explained, looking around for water.

"We can see that! Your hair's all . . . crazy!" The digs were really starting to get to me now, and the annoying thing was, I could see it in her face. The snide expression beneath the mask of lovely angelicness. I felt like I was the only one who could see it. Like she was some kind of goddess to all men, but as soon as a woman got close she could see that under the beauty lay hard, cold scales and claws. Just like Wes's mother! I suppressed a gasp. "D'ya want some agua?"

Off you, devil woman? No way!

"Or I've got some Coke here, if you want it?" offered Jonah. I took the Coke.

151

13

We sat under the tree's shade and chilled for another hour or so, until the bloke came on to the speaker and announced that there would be a performance break before the evening line-up started, so we trundled back over to the tent.

"I think I'm just going to go grab some food from over there." Jonah pointed to a Chinese truck. "Fancy something? I'll bring it back for you."

"Yeah, sure," I nodded. "Chow mein, please."

This was so weird. He kept on almost waiting on me, and being affectionate. It was starting to freak me out a bit, actually.

Wes, Emily and I dodged our way through the sights and smells of the food field – guys shouting left, right and centre for people to buy their gourmet, all of it smelling very, erm, *festivally*. Maybe I didn't want anything, on second thought.

I touched Wes's arm.

"I'm just going to go back and tell Jonah that I don't want anything, that I've changed my mind. I'll see you in a few."

I turned on my heel, and suddenly feeling a spurt of energy, I sprinted in and out of the crowd, over to the Chinese cart. The queue was long, but Jonah was nowhere to be seen in it. Just a lot of girls, some weird goth-boys, some people with so much hair that I couldn't see if they were girls or boys, and a black-haired boy and a redhead girl kissing about halfway down the line. I scanned it again, looking for Jonah. He should have been about where the kissing couple were by now, because the line was moving quite quickly. I was just about to turn around when the couple turned, so I got a profile view of their faces instead of the back of the girl's head.

It was only Jonah.

My heart skipped a beat.

I took a better look.

Yep, definitely him, lip ring and all.

For a second, I felt numb. I felt like a complete and utter fool. I thought I was going to cry. He'd used me – he'd used me for a place to stay the night because he knew that I would do anything for him.

But, wait – would I?

I thought about it.

No, I would have done anything for him about a week and a half before, but since then. . .

153

No.

I didn't like Jonah Jones.

So where were all these feelings coming from? All of the tight tummy feelings, the feeling sick and excited and miserable at the same time, and the jealousy, the one I'd do anything for—

Then it all clicked.

Looking back, it took me long enough.

I ran back to the tent, hardly seeing what I was doing or where I was going. I smashed into a boy blindly, who shouted after me like a crazy man, but I didn't stop. I didn't stop until I got back to the tent, and I threw open the flap.

"Wes?" I cried, gasping from the run.

Emily appeared. "He's not here, he's gone to talk to a friend. What's up? You must be really unfit. You're panting like Paris Hilton's puppy."

"Oh, only I've seen Jonah getting off with some red-haired ho instead of me! Good times."

She didn't even bat an eyelid. "So what if he's kissing some other chick. You two weren't exclusive."

Her honeyed tones were gone. So was the angelic face. The shadow of the tent gave an ugly glint to her pixie features.

Suddenly it didn't matter if I was nice to her or not any more.

"Y'know what, Barbie, I've had it up to here –" I held up my hand to my head. "– with you being a snidey little biatch with me –"

"I'm sorry, up to where?" she asked, mockingly.

She was really pushing my patience. I carried on.

154

"– and I don't know why, because I've set you up here – I got you some nice friends, a nice scene and a nice guy –"

She snorted and walked out into the middle of the tent, about to push open the flap at the front like she was bored.

"Yeah, and that's what he is, a *nice guy*! There's nothing there! He's not buff, he's cute – he's not dark, he's, ugrh, *witty* – and y'know what? He's boring! He's a geek! He's got some serious money, though—"

But I didn't get to hear the rest of the sentence, because I'd grabbed her arm and used all of my tiny body strength to push her straight out of the open tent door, sending her sprawling on to the grass. How dare she speak about Wes like he wasn't worth her time! He may be cute, he may be witty and he may be a geek, but that's Wes! That's what makes him so great, and special and unique and—

I threw open the flap, livid, just in time to see Wes rush to her side, his expression one of deep concern.

"Get that crazy girl away from me!" screamed Emily. Somehow she had managed to burst into tears. Nice touch. She started to shake too. "Wes, she's been bullying me ever since I came here! She calls me names and threatens me, she's so jealous! Get her away from me, please!"

And for a big exit, she gave me a tremulous, wide-eyed, teary glance, like a terrified rabbit, and took off into the sea of tents without a backward glance.

Evil, conniving, cow-faced—

"What the hell, Holly?" Wes exploded. "Did you just *push* her? This isn't like you. What the hell do you think you're playing at?!"

Overwhelmed, I shouted back. "Yeah, well, I did, but Wes, she's not the girl you think she is!" I exclaimed. "She's the one who's been bullying me! She's the one who's been making snide comments! She's just said all this stuff about how you're boring and not right for her, but something about you having a load of cash—"

"Enough!" he shouted. "What are you trying to do! Why are you trying to ruin this? Just because you've got *Jonah* now doesn't mean you can do whatever the hell you please—"

"I just found Jonah sucking the face of some red-haired bimbo!" I cried, still only vaguely aware of the many pairs of eyes upon us. "So it's nothing to do with him."

He paused for a second, taking in the new information, and I almost thought he was going to feel sorry for me.

"Are you sure it's nothing to do with him?" he shot back venomously. "Aren't you just trying to sabotage this so that you won't be alone again? Aren't you just jealous?"

"Of course I'm jealous!" I blurted out before I could stop myself. "She has *you*! And *I'm* supposed to be the one who has you – *me*, not *her* – because it's *me* who actually likes you, it's *me* who actually—"

I couldn't finish the sentence. Not in front of all those people. Not with him looking at me like that, like I was something nasty trodden into his precious tent. Not with Jonah walking back towards us, laden with Chinese food—

I ran for it in the opposite direction, not looking back, not daring to do anything – apart from run and run and run, until there was no more space to run in to.

14

Lie under the stars, in my arms tonight
And I'll tell you that we'll be all right.
But if you whisper a lie to my heart tonight
It won't be OK,
It won't be all right.

I sat with my back to the fence, listening to the song.

I didn't know how long I had been sat there. I did know that it was getting dark, and that the temperature was dropping, and that I'd left my jacket back at the tent.

Stupid girl.

I was a stupid, stupid girl.

How did I manage to get into this mess?

I thought hard. Oh yes, it was about the same time I promised Wes that if a girl walked into Ozzie's that he really wanted, I would help him take her to MSR with us, in our tent.

And now I was there, sat with my back to the cold fence, having the most miserable time of my life, when I was supposed to be having the best. I'd toyed with the idea of getting Mum or Dad to come and pick me up, but cleverly I had dropped my mobile into the tent when we had gone back, and I wasn't about to go back for it now. And I'd got this far, I was here at the gig – why should I leave? I wanted to see my band play on a huge stage in front of hundreds of people, hearing them scream and feeling them surge, having that feeling of being involved in something bigger than me, bigger than Wes, bigger than the whole situation – I was craving that right now. I needed the music to calm my soul again. And I needed it fast.

From where I was sitting, I could just about hear the speakers. Some band was on who had a good strong beat to their music. Wes would like them. Maybe he would be there now, dancing like I showed him, dancing with the no-good, evil, blonde. . .

I couldn't even bring myself to muster up a decent insult.

I shoved my iPod back into my ears and put it on to shuffle.

Familiar notes.

Drums.

Bass.

"*Love in idleness. . .*" I whispered to myself, ironically.

If there was one thing that I'd learnt those past two weeks?

There is definitely nothing idle about falling in love.

I watched the sky as the midsummer moon shone bright, even though it wasn't quite fully dark yet. It shone like a beacon down on me. I suddenly had the cheesy thought of wondering how many people were looking at the same moon right then and there, and how many of those people were sat feeling miserable like me.

The next thing I knew I was being shaken awake. I must have dozed off, looking at the sky. A big, black, bushy mane was shaking in my face, and I jumped out of my skin because I thought I was being attacked by a huge dog. As I jumped up, my head collided with a shoulder, sending me crashing back down into the grass again, accompanied by a squeal of pain.

Ahh, déjà-vu!

"Well, darling, she is not unconscious! That is always a good start."

The hand of the shaggy dog reached down into my vision and hauled me on to my feet with ease. The helper then backed away and I saw that it was Finn, with Margo stood behind him, arms crossed. She had lost the shades and her hair was tied back. Margo never ties her hair back. I looked a little closer and saw that her arms were slightly pink from sunburn, and she was smiling.

And not even a crocodile smile –

– but an actual smile.

A smile which had a faint resemblance to Wes's cheeky grin, a shadow of his humour and humanity; it was all there in her small, genuine smile.

She stepped forward and I saw that she also wasn't wearing any make-up. Not that she needed it, she was gorgeous anyway, but still. It was like she was at one with herself, like she'd decided that her bum was sore from riding up on her high horse day in, day out, and just decided to get down, be herself.

I was a little scared, actually.

"What are you doing, Holly?" she asked, without even a trace of a sneer.

"Well, I was sitting. . ." I started shakily, not quite knowing how to react. "And now, I guess I'm standing."

"No," she said calmly. "I meant, what are you doing *here*?"

She gestured to the back end of the field and the fence.

I looked around, but only saw what a mess I had made of the situation. I couldn't say all the stuff that had just happened; I just couldn't relive the moment right away.

"It doesn't matter," I mumbled, turning away. "You wouldn't understand."

"If you tried us, you might be surprised."

A low, slow voice had spoken those words. The voice sounded . . . wise, so that I stopped and listened. I turned around to see Finn push his fringe out of his eyes to look at me. They were like cat's eyes – cut like glass, all amber and deep, like they were pouring into my soul just a little bit.

Jeez, no wonder he covered those bad boys up.

But something in his voice compelled me to speak.

"Jonah kissed some other girl. Emily was a bitch to me, looking down on me and saying horrible stuff. I pushed her. Wes came up. I told him that she had been a cow and that she wasn't

160

to be trusted. Wes took her side, and now he hates me. What else is there to say?"

"Darling," Margo said, her brown eyes surveying my face. "This is the only time I will ever offer you my advice, so listen closely: do not go around with boys who think with their trousers. Do not mix with girls who switch boys faster than they switch their underwear. And most importantly—" she smiled knowingly, "do not try to fix up your best friend with a girl who clearly is just a replacement for the someone that they truly want. Said best friend is obviously far too afraid to talk to the person he likes, just in case he loses her as a friend, and it ruins their friendship for ever."

She stepped forward and whispered into my ear.

"Take it from an outsider who *knows*," she said. "He couldn't ever hate you, Holly. He loves you too much."

She backed away, and Finn took her hand. I'd never seen them hold hands before. Ever. Something had changed. As I took in a deep breath, I felt it. In the ebony night air, all my senses had come alive and I felt peaceful: it was almost like Margo had done something to the air herself, like she'd worked some magic and everything just became clear and right.

"It's nearly half past eleven, Holly," Margo said softly. "Shouldn't you get going?"

I didn't need telling twice.

I ran through a ghost town of empty tents; everyone had obviously left already to get to the show. I ran through the stalls and vendors, who were still awake, dodging staff and random passers-by – it was all a blur, but as I reached the opening of the field I came to a halt. It was heaving. All I could see were bodies – bodies milling around, talking, waiting, dancing to the now-quieter speaker music. I wasn't going to get through. It just wasn't going to happen. The announcement just said that it was 11.35 p.m. It seemed impossible that I could navigate my way around the crowd to the front by the time it started; there was just no way.

I absentmindedly fiddled with my wrist, and looked down at the purple bracelet on it.

Pit pass.

Ozzie.

Wes.

I ran into the maze of people, and started to frantically work my way through. I couldn't tell where I was going, I couldn't see a thing – it felt like I was going around and around in circles, seeing the same T-shirts, the same hairstyles, the same songs being sung all around. It was like those funhouses where there are mirrors all around and you can't find the exit through a sea of your own reflections staring back at you from every possible angle.

I cursed myself for being so short. I couldn't see a thing, and I started to panic, and my breathing started to go. I staggered forward, trying to block out the feeling of being trapped and isolated; the feeling that was bearing down on my chest like a cage constricting, around my lungs, and squeezing them until they were sore. I picked up a bit of speed, getting desperate to escape, but my foot got caught in a hole in the ground and I crashed into a girl in front of me.

I apologized the best I could through my gasping breaths and hauled myself back up as she asked if I was all right. I only vaguely heard her as I tried to look through the people for the gate. Then someone grabbed my arm and spun me around. I was face to face with Jack, lip ring and all. I smiled humourlessly. I think I've gone off lip rings – permanently.

"Holly, are you all right? I saw you fall."

I nodded, breathing in a deep breath. Seeing him, even though he was still a complete stranger, was comforting. The crowd wasn't a huge sea of faceless people; they were real, I wasn't trapped. . .

The suffocating paranoia of claustrophobia faded.

"I'm fine," I burbled. "I'm just trying to find the pit gate. I need to get to the pit because I need to get there before the set; I need to get there to find my –"

I paused, frowning, and then reluctantly finished the sentence.

"– friend."

"Was he the guy at the bar with you? He turned up eventually?" he asked with a wry smile.

I smiled back. "It turned out he'd been there all the time – I just hadn't seen him."

Jack nodded, lips drawn in tight. Then he smiled easily and pointed to our right.

"Just over there is the pit entrance. It's nearly twelve, though, so you'd better run if you want to find your *friend.*"

"Thank you," I smiled, and turned away. Then on a sudden impulse, I shouted back over my shoulder. "I owe you a drink, Jack, I won't forget!"

163

I heard his laugh melt into the crowd as I finally hit the pit, waved my purple band in the guard's face, and entered. I saw straight away that there would be no point in trying to look for Wes – the people were packed like sardines. My heart dropped. I was too late. . .

Then an almighty chord echoed over the crowd, and I saw Matt crouching down with his guitar on the left-hand side of the stage as I looked at it, making sure he was in tune. The electrical buzz zinged through me. I just had to get to where he was – I just *had* to.

Now was the time to play my short-person card: being little is sometimes the best thing at a gig, because you can just slide through the gaps. So I did. I managed to sqeeze right through, right to the front, right to the bar next to the steps where the bands walk on to the stage.

And there was Matt's perfect bum right in front of me; about three metres away, and up on the stage. It was calling to me! I suddenly had the urge to pinch it, but I just wasn't close enough. . .

He stood up and turned around to face the audience. He did a small wave with his guitar, and the crowd just erupted into screams and shouts and cries. He had a small, sheepish grin on his face, like he still couldn't believe that after three years people were screaming to see him. But we were. He was an icon – the lyric-writer of the band. Wes loved him for that, being a poetry geek and everything. And of course he was wearing his first-ever guitar. In all of his interviews, all he'd talked about was his guitar – the black, smooth, rounded curves of the base;

he loved that guitar "more than any woman he had ever met". Being so close, I saw that it had more dents than paint – it was a wonder it was still playing right, after he'd played it at every show without fail. He'd made it a part of his performance – the guitar was as much of an icon as he was, and he liked to say that it "spawned a god", but personally, I feel that the god was already there: his amazing riffs just started something magical.

Then I thought I was going to explode! I jumped on to the fence (my ultra-small feet could fit through the holes) so that I was higher up than other people and I had an amazing view. At that point, Chevans walked on to the stage with his cocky swagger, swinging his drumsticks around his fingers and sitting at his drum kit. Like before every gig, he spun around twice on his stool, clicked out his fingers, then winked at the audience and gave us a little bit of hi-hat action. Once again, we all went wild. I thought I was going to get crushed as the people behind started to surge forward, but the pressure only made me scream louder and more passionately as Vikki strutted on to the stage with her violently pink bass, looking amazing in a small tartan skirt and bright turquoise top – her hair bleach blonde with green and pink through it, her nose pierced with a ring and make-up fierce. Then came the moment that everyone had been waiting for.

A voice came over the speakers: a deep, husky, bad-boy voice that made my limbs melt and my head explode.

"*The iron tongue of midnight hath told twelve*
Lovers, to bed—"

And out walked the spokesman for every confused teenager on the planet.

Robin Goodfellow smiled broodily at the audience, radiating a godly glow that made me feel sick with pleasure. Ever the performer, he cocked an eyebrow at us, and finished his set-up line.

"'Tis almost Faerie time. . .!"

And so came the screams from all around me, deafening, but they couldn't drown out the song.

Robin pointed to Matt, and in came the tune.

"You're the riff that starts this story. . ."

Chevans, drums and symbols.

"You're the drums, your one song glory. . ."

Vikki stroking that bass.

"This song, your song, our song, its true"

Silence.

"'Cause everything is idle when it's done for – STOP! Stop, wait – no, sorry!"

All the rest of the band stopped what they were doing and looked up. The crowd started to reply in outrage; I shouted along with the rest. What were they playing at?

"What!" cried Vikki. "What are you doing?"

Robin ran over and talked rapidly to her. Her eyes flicked around the audience, and I could have sworn she looked straight at me for a second, but I couldn't tell, and then Robin ran off to speak to Chevans, and Vikki spoke to Matt.

"What's going on?!" someone nearby shouted, and Robin looked up at the audience, grinned, and then resumed his place centre stage.

166

"I'm sorry, guys, we just can't play this song until . . . we get some people up on stage here with us."

The sea of teenagers suddenly loved him again, and every hand stretched high into the air; the screaming was battering my eardrums and I could hardly breathe let alone scream from the pushing behind me in a rush to get to the front. I grabbed on to the fencing for support and gasped as the air was rammed out of me, and I watched painfully as Robin ran down from the stage into the gap between stage and fence, and walked along the row. Screaming girls were leaning over to touch him, and he walked straight past me to the middle of the section, as Vikki went to the other end. Everyone was lurching forward, stretching out, but he didn't pick anyone. He surveyed the faces with a glowing smile on his dark features, and then clocked my eyes from about three metres away, and I knew that he knew who I was. I almost died. He knew me. Robin knew me. And he'd picked me. Oh my god, he'd picked me, yes, he was nodding and pointing at me—

"Her." He said to the nearest security guards, and before I knew it I was being lifted out of the crowd and on to the steps, ready to go on stage with the band.

My band.

Oh my God.

I thought my legs were going to give way, but I took slow, even strides up the stairs and into the light. It was so bright that I had to shield my eyes for a moment to get used to the glare. Then I felt a hand take my elbow to guide me across the stage. I looked at its owner.

Only Robin.

I would have fainted, but then I caught sight of the audience, and it just took my breath away.

Hundreds of people, shouting and screaming, taking photos and smiling and waving; people on other people's shoulders, people jumping up and down—

Just so many people.

All in one space.

All in one field.

All waiting to hear a piece of music that I had been pulled on stage to witness with the best band of all time.

Matt picked up the riff, Chevans the drums, Vikki the bass, and they kept a round going where they had left off. I was still awestruck by the audience, and was only vaguely aware that Robin was talking over the music.

". . . and this is a special song for some special people. Some people who make the effort to support us as much as they can . . ."

I scanned the crowd for any faces I knew.

". . . came to most of the tour, just to see us play the same set time and time again . . ."

I couldn't see anyone.

". . . they make a really cute couple, don't you think?"

Was that Wes down there at the front?!

". . . so let's sing it along for them, shall we. . .?"

No, my eyes were playing tricks on me. It wasn't him, it was some other—

And that was when millions of tiny shimmery shreds of plastic, almost like confetti, rained from above me. It was unbelievable. All of the light hit the various colours, and made the entire stage feel like a different world, like I was suspended in time. It was so beautiful that I staggered backwards in surprise, as Robin began to sing with what sounded like the whole of the audience as backing:

"'*Cause everything is idle when it's done for –*"

I bumped into something and spun around fast.

"*– you!*"

Straight into Wes.

The music carried on playing. Robin carried on singing. The confetti carried on falling. The crowd carried on screaming.

Wes took my hand and looked at me with those big conker eyes like he hadn't seen me in years.

"It turns out that American blondes and bad-ass English boys rather like each other. . ." he shouted, so that I could hear him. "Margo knew all along, but only told me now because she 'didn't want to stir'."

Ironic much?

"But I just saw him with some redhead!" I cried, bemused.

He laughed and shrugged. "Well then, he's even more of a jerk than I thought he was. He and Emily deserve each other."

"Well, maybe that's OK," I shouted back, determined for him to hear me over the amazing music. "Because that turns out to be a lot less hassle for me if she isn't with you!"

He smirked, holding up his hands in a surrendering pose.

"Less hassle?" he yelled sarcastically. "I can't expect anything to be idle when it's done for you!"

I grinned, stepped up to him, and kissed him ever so lightly on his gorgeous lips ('cause there were hundreds of people watching, after all!). I kissed him again, softly, and just stayed there for a moment in his arms with confetti swirling around us like a glittery snowstorm. It was amazing, like a dream, and everything just felt . . . . right. Like I couldn't believe I'd wasted my time on other guys when Wes had been there all along. Then all the sound and colour rushed back and hit us full force. It suddenly came back to me – that we were on stage with our favourite band, with hundreds of people watching, and they were playing our song . . .

So we danced.

And I carried on smiling, and so did he; all through what was left of the perfect midsummer night's eve.